Midnight Realm

Anjalee Scott

For my mother who raised me on vampires and werewolves. Thanks, Mom.

Other Books by Anjalee:

The Arrangement

The Craving

Reckless

Masquerade – *coming December 2017*

https://anjaleescott.com

One
Wednesday April 5, 2017

It was a ten-hour flight from JFK to Venice, and Hannah's legs were stiff from the confines of her seat in the coach section. She'd hoped for first-class, but the Metropolitan Museum of Art wouldn't foot the bill, and she didn't want to eat through her personal savings. Thankfully, they were approaching the landing strip, and she would soon get to stretch her legs. While waiting for her turn to exit, she adjusted the time on her watch. According to the perky flight attendant, it was 3:38 p.m. Wednesday afternoon. She had one week to secure the rare necklace she was after and hopefully, fit in plenty of sightseeing before her trip back to New York. She filed off the jumbo jet behind the other passengers and made her way to the baggage claim area. Luckily, her suitcase was a hot pink designer brand and easy to spot on the conveyor belt.

She exchanged her money for Euros and hailed a water taxi at the nearest pier. With her bags in tow, and in shaky Italian, she instructed the driver to take her to the Locanda Orseolo Hotel. She stared across the water at the beautiful scenery of Venice and the people walking around Piazza San Marco. She couldn't wait to explore it for herself, but she would need a nap first to get her body on Italy time. Once she was checked into her luxurious room, she plopped down on the queen size bed and quickly drifted off into a dreamless sleep.

She woke up at 6:00 p.m., feeling refreshed and famished. The food served on the jet lacked flavor and wasn't enough to satisfy, so an authentic Italian dinner would be a welcomed delight.

She changed into a light pant suit, to fit the spring-like weather, and a pair of flats before twisting her long blond hair up into a hair claw. She freshened up her makeup, put in a dainty set of pearl earrings that her last love had given her, and left to walk around the piazza. Piazza San Marco, known to Americans as St. Mark's Square, was alive with culture and various aromas coming from quaint restaurants and pubs. Hannah had studied the area before her trip and had decided the first place she'd dine would be Tuttinpiedi.

When she entered the charming establishment, the delicious scents of cheese and garlic wafted to her. A lovely hostess, dressed in a red blouse and colorful skirt, promptly seated her at a table for two and then removed the extra place setting. Hannah felt a pang of sorrow as she contemplated being in such a beautiful and romantic city alone. It would've been nice to have someone to share the trip with, not to mention the nights back home, but she'd broken up with her boyfriend of three years several months ago and hadn't sought out the company of another man since. She still had feelings for Rick, but the relationship wasn't heading where she wanted and needed it to go. She was already twenty-nine and wanted to get married and start a family, but that didn't seem to be on his agenda. When she'd called off the relationship, she thought it would get him on the same page, but he had accepted her dismissal with only a frown and a couple of tears. It had made her wonder if he'd really loved her or just the idea of her.

Hannah shook her head to get Rick out of her mind and resumed perusing her menu. Luckily, she had her English-Italian dictionary with her to decipher it. She was still cross-referencing when the server returned. He was a handsome young Italian man with dark hair and eyes and smooth olive colored skin. He gave her a kind smile and gestured to the menu.

In fluent English, thick with his Italian accent, he asked her, "Have you decided on what to have for dinner, mademoiselle?"

Hannah smiled sheepishly and felt herself blush from embarrassment. "Well, I'd like to have lasagna, but I can't find it on the menu."

The server, whose name was Roberto according to the nametag he wore, chuckled softly and pointed it out on the menu. "It is here under entrees," he said, and she saw it was right under her nose the entire time.

"Thank you. I'll have that with a house salad and some garlic rolls, please." She handed the menu back to him.

"And for your drink, may I recommend the house wine?" he inquired.

Normally, Hannah didn't drink, but she was sort of on vacation, so she chimed, "Certainly."

"Very good. I'll bring it with your meal, so the flavors can complement one another," he suggested, and she gave him a polite nod.

When he walked away, she looked around the establishment at the other patrons until she felt jealous pangs again. Then she got out her dictionary and studied for her meeting at the Accademia Museum in the morning. As the lead curator for the Metropolitan Museum of Art, she was on a mission to secure a priceless necklace featuring a four-and-a-half carat red diamond surrounded by smaller white diamonds. The red diamond by itself was valued at one million dollars per carat and was the second largest red diamond in the world—only one-point-six carats smaller than the Moussaieff Red Diamond. She had been instructed by her employers to negotiate a price of no more than five-and-a-half million dollars to acquire the piece. She'd never made a large offer like that before, so to say her nerves were on edge, would be an understatement.

After cleaning most of her plate and downing two glasses of Chardonnay, Hannah was ready to explore the quaint shops in the plaza. After all, she couldn't possibly go home without a pair of genuine Italian leather shoes or a new purse, even though her closet was already overflowing with accessories. *Maybe I'll just window shop. Yeah right.*

Street musicians were playing instruments varying from accordions and wooden flutes to steel drums all along the sidewalk, creating an atmosphere of excitement. A flower vendor approached her with two bouquets of blossoms in vibrant hues, and before she could deny him the sale, she was reaching for her wallet. She chose the assortment with the most pinks and then turned to continue down the sidewalk.

"Grazie!" the vendor called out after her.

Her next stop was the Gucci store. She promised herself she'd just look around, but she left with a $3,500 charge to her credit card for a pink leather shoulder bag and white patent leather sandals. *There's my first-class ticket right there.* It was a good thing she'd recently received a raise.

With her purchases securely clutched in her hands, she walked back to the hotel and turned in for the night. Her meeting with the Accademia Museum curators was set for 8:00 in the morning, so she arranged for a wake-up call at 6:00. Her room overlooked the Orseolo canal, and the sound of the water lapping against the bricks lulled her to sleep.

Two
Thursday

Hannah woke up at 5:30, so she canceled her wake-up call and took a quick shower. She had a small deck off her suite, and it made a perfect spot for her have a light breakfast. She used her smartphone to check her email and the local weather report. It was going to be a sunny spring day, so she dressed in a pink A-line skirt with a white blouse and her new sandals.

At 7:30, she hailed a taxi to take her to the Accademia Museum for her meeting. A folder, which contained a procurement contract, was safely tucked underneath her arm, and she secured her new pink leather bag close to her body. The sidewalks and canals of Venice were already bustling with the locals and tourists alike. She saw two large posters advertising the grand opening of a new exhibit at the museum and wondered if that is what was drawing some of the crowd.

She stepped inside the expansive gallery and was immediately greeted by a security officer. He was checking purses and sending people through metal detectors. In shaky Italian, Hannah explained to the man that she was a curator for the Metropolitan Museum of Art, and she was there for a meeting with the director and registrar.

The guard replied in rapid Italian until she looked up at him with a blank expression. Then in English, he told her, "I'm sorry. Your Italian was quite good, so I thought you spoke it fluently."

Hannah shook her head. "I'm just learning it."

He gave her a pleasant smile and said, "You're learning it well." Then he pointed toward the winding staircase in the corner of the room. "Mr. Fabrizio and Miss

Giacomo are waiting for you in the main office. It's the first room on the right in the hallway after the stairs. I'll call ahead and tell them you're here. Enjoy Italy!"

The closed door swung open just as Hannah reached it. A short man with olive toned skin stepped out of the massive office and extended a warm hand to her. A dark-haired robust woman of equal height followed him. Hannah expected a handshake from her too, but the woman pulled her in for a surprising hug and kiss on both cheeks.

She must've jerked away harder than she realized because the older woman apologized, "Ecco come ci salutiamo in Italia."

Diego Fabrizio, the museum's director, laughed when Hannah pulled out her Italian dictionary. To Maria Giacomo, the registrar, he said, "In English, Maria."

The woman blushed along with Hannah. "I'm sorry. I said that's how we greet each other in Italy."

Hannah waved her off. "It's okay. I want to learn the language and customs."

"How long is your stay in our charming city?" Diego inquired while gesturing for her to take one of the leather chairs in the impressive office.

Hannah looked around the room at the ornate décor. There were tapestries in rich reds, greens, and purples. Antiques lined mahogany shelves, and paintings decorated each wall.

"I leave next Wednesday," she answered.

"Oh, well, you definitely must dine with us this evening. We can discuss the places you simply must see while here," he told her with robust enthusiasm.

"Yes, that's a wonderful idea!" Maria chimed in and clasped Hannah's arm. "We'll take you to the Riviera for a fine meal."

Hannah had wanted to do some sightseeing that evening, but she found their hopeful expressions impossible to decline. "Sure. That sounds delightful."

Diego clapped his hands together. "Great! It's settled then. You can meet us here at 7:00. Now, let's get down to business, shall we?"

Butterflies churned in Hannah's stomach. This was a big moment in her career. "Can I see the necklace?"

"Oh, si! I'll go get it for you now," Diego told her.

After he left the room, Hannah realized her knee was bobbing wildly. She placed her hand on it to stop the jerking.

Maria caught the movement out of the corner of her eye and smiled. "It's a big purchase for you, si?"

Hannah felt the warmth in her cheeks, and her voice trembled as much as her knee. "Yes, it's a big move for me and for the museum. It will be a highlighted piece for us."

Maria nodded vigorously. "Si, it's a majestic piece. It will bring in massive crowds."

Escorted by a pair of armed security guards, Diego returned then with a black velvet case. He closed the office door behind him and clicked both locks. He smiled sheepishly at Hannah and glanced at the doorknob.

"You can't be too careful with such a rare item. Like America, our beautiful country has thieves."

Hannah nodded while staring at the closed velvet box. "Oh, I understand completely. I'm actually wondering how I'm going to get it back to my hotel safely."

He waved one hand at her. "Oh, no, no, no. You need not worry. My armed guards will escort you, and we will contact the hotel manager to be certain it is locked up in the hotel safe. I don't trust the safes in rooms; I hope you understand."

"I do. I understand completely, and our insurance is set to go into effect on it the moment it is acquired." She placed the file folder in her lap and opened it to retrieve the document. "It's all written into the contract."

"Let me show you the necklace then," he said with a happy sigh. "It will take your breath away. Pictures simply do not do her justice."

He opened the case, and she squealed in awe. The stunning antique necklace was the most captivating piece she'd ever seen. The enormous red diamond glowed like a fire, capturing the sunlight streaming into the room and reflecting it into a thousand points.

"It's unbelievable!" Hannah shrieked. "It's gorgeous." She reached for the box, but quickly withdrew her hand. "May I?"

"Si, of course; she is to be yours," Diego said with an amused grin.

Hannah accepted the velvet box and stared in admiration. "It's remarkable. It must be at least six hundred years old."

"Actually, we calculate her to be between seven hundred and eight hundred years old. She was discovered in Egypt according to her oldest records, which will accompany her," Maria explained.

"That's amazing," Hannah said and lightly touched the brilliant stone with her fingertip.

The room began to shake, and she almost dropped the box as she clutched the edges of the deep chair. Diego lunged under his desk, and Maria balled up on the floor with her hands clasped over her neck. It was an earthquake. It only lasted about twelve seconds, but it felt like hours, and she'd never been in one before.

When the tremors subsided, Diego rushed to the window and shouted, "Come. Look!"

Hannah and Maria both scrambled to see what he was pointing at, and they immediately saw it. There was an avalanche rolling down the side of the Dolomites Mountains. The windows vibrated yet, but the floor was mercifully still.

What they couldn't see from their location was a cavern on the side of the mountain where red eyes opened for the first time in over four hundred years.

Three

"Well, that was exciting. I go on vacation and end up in an earthquake," Hannah remarked.

Diego bobbed his head. "Sadly, they are common here."

"Si, but not the avalanche," Maria added quietly and then shot a look of concern to Diego. "Do you suppose…"

"No, no, no. That's just a legend, Maria," he interrupted. He shook his head and waved a hand at her.

Hannah was confused. "What legend?"

Diego shrugged with a forced smile. "It's an ancient story that comes with the necklace."

Her face lit up. "Oh, please tell me. I love European history and legends."

He gestured to her chair, so she sat back down. He sat in his desk chair, and Maria sat in the one to Hannah's right. He took a sip of water and cleared his throat.

"The legend goes back to Egypt. It was believed that Anubis, god of the dead, created an immortal creature when he fell in love with a human soul and transported her back to earth. She, in turn, created other immortals to pay homage to the god. However, when Anubis had a falling out with Isis, the goddess of protection, she smote the immortals, including his love, and had her husband, Osiris, who was also Anubis's father, damn the souls back to the underworld.

"The humans created an amulet to pay homage to Isis for her protection, and she blessed it to keep them safe."

Hannah's jaw dropped. "Are you talking about *vampires?*"

He wore a sheepish grin and slowly nodded. "Si, that is what man chose to call them."

"And this is the magical amulet?" She asked and pointed to the red diamond necklace.

"Si," Maria answered before Diego could.

Hannah pursed her lips. "Interesting story. I like it"—she turned to face Maria—"You started to say something earlier about the legend."

Maria's round cheeks turned red. "I am just wondering if the necklace…um…Oh, never mind. I'm just a foolish old woman," she said and waved it off.

Diego clapped his hands together. "So, let's see what your contract says in the way of an offer."

Hannah showed him the paperwork, which would authorize an automatic payment from the Met as soon as she faxed it to the museum director with Diego and Maria's signatures.

Diego ran a hand through his thick hair and sighed. "I was hoping for six million." He stood and paced the elegant office.

"Well, you see it in print that five-and-a-half is the most they'll spend," she pointed out. "I was advised that under no circumstances would that be negotiable."

He looked down at the paper again and rubbed a hand across his jaw. "Well, since you had to suffer through one of our quakes, I'll accept their offer," he finally said and signed on the dotted line.

He passed the document to Maria, who signed her name without reading the contract over. "We can fax it in right now," she said as she rose from her chair. She showed the signatures to Hannah and then put it in the fax machine, which was resting on a smaller desk in the corner. "It should only take a minute to go through."

Diego was straightening items on his shelves that had shifted during the earthquake. "You'd be surprised by how many times I have to straighten this stuff up. I should just glue it down," he commented with a grimace.

The fax machine beeped once and printed the confirmation page. "It successfully sent, and here's your hardcopy," Maria said while handing over the signed contract.

"Don't you want to copy it for your records?" Hannah asked.

Maria threw her hands up. "Si, yes. I must be scatterbrained from the quake." She took the papers back and ran them through a copy machine which stood next to the fax machine. The copier quickly scanned and printed the pages out. "Now, I think I'm all done with them," she remarked and handed them off to Hannah once more.

"Terrific. Is there anything else?" Hannah inquired while admiring the necklace again.

Diego looked up from straightening the contents of his desk. "Si, meet us at 7:00 for dinner. You'll have a magnificent time! As you Americans say, we know how to party."

She laughed and told them, "Certainly. I'd love to dine with you."

"Wonderful. Now, the armed guards outside the door will escort you back to the Locanda Orseolo Hotel. If you like, though, Maria will go too."

She waved his suggestion off. "No, that won't be necessary. I'll be fine."

Diego escorted her to the door and spoke in rapid Italian to the guards. "Antonio speaks a little English in case you have any questions," he explained and pointed to the taller guard.

"Grazie," she replied in Italian since it was one word she knew. "I'm at the Locanda Orseolo," she explained slowly to the guard.

Both guards nodded, and Antonio gently gripped her arm after she secured the necklace case in her purse.

She looked back at Diego with a smile. "I hope no one thinks I'm being escorted off the premises for causing trouble."

He and Maria laughed and waved goodbye. "Until we see you later," he called out.

It took only twenty-eight minutes to get back to her room after the necklace was secured by the hotel manager in the large safe. Just to cover her bases, she had Mr. Cortez sign a document assuring the necklace's safety.

She called the Met and spoke to her supervisor to confirm they received the fax and that the insurance documents were in place. She was told everything was good to go and not to worry.

Oh sure. And how many priceless heirlooms are you going to be toting around?

She lay down for a nap, so she'd be rested for shopping and then dinner with Maria and Diego afterward. As she tried to fall asleep, she replayed the tale of vampires that accompanied the necklace. It led to disturbing dreams.

Four

Hannah's phone alarm woke her up at 1:30 p.m. She sat on the balcony with a tour guide brochure to read over while eating a pastrami sandwich that room service brought up. She used her ink pen to circle the evening gondola ride, wondering if she could convince Diego and Maria to accompany her. She didn't mind going alone, but it would be nice to have someone to talk to and help point out the sights.

An hour later, she left the hotel and walked through more of Piazza San Marco. She browsed the shops for gifts to take back home to her family and friends. While looking at bracelets for her sister, she came across a pair of red ruby earrings that caught her eye, and they reminded her of the beautiful necklace. She looked down at the red dress she was wearing and purchased the earrings along with a stunning bracelet for her sister, Joanne. She slipped the earrings on before leaving the store. Her next stop was at the Fendi store. She knew her mother wouldn't approve of a lavish present, but she bought her a nice wallet anyway. She'd just rip off the tag and tell her that it was on clearance. She also purchased a dress shirt and silk tie for her father.

Hannah didn't find anything for her two best friends yet, but she had several days to keep looking. She hailed a taxi to take her purchases back to her hotel room, leaving her just enough time to freshen up and make her way to the museum by 7:00.

The Riviera was bustling with patrons when they arrived. Hannah ordered the chicken parmesan because of Diego's recommendation, and it was delicious. They shared a bottle of Merlot and toasted to the deal they had made that morning.

"To your success," Diego cheered, and he and Maria held their glasses up.

"To yours," Hannah replied and raised hers too.

Shortly after the toast, Diego received a phone call summoning him home for a family emergency.

"I hope everything is all right," Hannah told him.

"I have an unruly teen who thinks he must act out every other day," he returned. "But we love him." He shrugged and left money for the bill. "This is enough to cover your meals, another bottle of wine, and the tip. Please stop by and see us again before you go home next week." He bowed his head in respect and left.

Hannah turned to Maria after their host was gone. "Can you tell me anything else about the legend of the necklace?"

She smiled and whispered, "Do you believe?"

Hannah scowled and reflexively fingered one of the ruby earrings. "Do I believe the story?"

Maria nodded, causing strands of black hair to come loose from her bun. "Si. Do you believe in"—she looked around them to make certain no one was eavesdropping—"the undead?"

Hannah smiled and took a sip of her wine. "No. I like watching scary movies, but I don't believe that monsters exist." She saw the woman frown, so she added, "Apparently, you must be a believer."

Maria blushed and nodded. "My family comes from a long line of Gypsies. Our people believe in magical creatures—especially the evil ones."

Hannah tilted her head. "Creatures plural? What else besides vampires?"

"Well…werewolves, witches, and demons to name a few."

Hannah's jaw dropped. "Wow. I had no idea cultures still believed in such things."

"Si, our culture is very rich in the knowledge of other beings. It's part of our history." She reached in her blouse and pulled out a talisman shaped like an eye with a blue gem in the center. "That's why I wear this. It's called a cat's eye, and it wards off black magic, spirits, and the evil eye."

"It's pretty," Hannah acknowledged with a smile. "Is it a family heirloom?"

"Si," Maria said and nodded for exclamation. "It was passed down from my great-grandmother."

Hannah pointed to a delicate gold filigree ring she wore on her right hand. "This was passed down to me from my grandmother."

Maria took her hand to admire the jewelry. "It's charming."

"Thank you," Hannah replied with a yawn. "Sorry about that. I guess I'm not adjusted to the time change yet."

Maria softly chuckled and patted her hand. "I understand, and I'm sleepy myself. It has been a rather eventful day for us."

Hannah nodded. "Indeed. I want to take a gondola ride and then go to bed. Maybe the rocking boat will help me sleep well tonight," she said with a laugh.

"I imagine it will. I wish you a good evening then, and as Diego said earlier, please see us again before you head back to the USA."

They both rose to leave, and Maria gave her a kiss on both cheeks.

"Grazie," Hannah told her before they parted ways.

She stepped out into the crisp air and was grateful that her dress was long enough to cover most of her legs. She followed a crowd of tourists to the small dock to wait on a gondola.

She had to wait for the second gondola because the first one quickly filled up. She boarded behind an elderly couple and took a seat in the rear. She was looking down at the black water, hypnotized by the lights that were dancing on its glassy surface, and she only looked up when she felt someone sit down next to her. It was an attractive Italian man.

"Excuse me, may I sit here? All the other seats are full," he explained in English.

She forced a smile while wondering if that was true since she hadn't been paying attention while the boat loaded.

She was about to say something, but his smile stopped her. "I'm sorry. That's not entirely true. I wanted to sit with you," he confessed.

She felt at a loss for words. Rick was the last man who flirted with her. "Why?" she finally voiced.

He smiled again. "Well, I see a lot of tourists from all over the world, but you caught my eye more than any other before you."

"Why?" she repeated and expected another cheesy pick-up line.

He shrugged. "Psychic ability runs in my family, and there is something about you that draws me in."

She leveled her gaze on him, noticing that he had full lips, and told him, "Well, that's one I haven't heard before."

He laughed, causing heads to turn their way. "I was going for originality, so score." He extended his hand for a shake. "Allow me to introduce myself. I'm Valentino Aleron."

She took his hand with a sliver of hesitation and was surprised by how warm and smooth his skin was. "It's nice to meet you, Valentino. My name is Hannah Rowen, and I'm, obviously, not from here."

He studied her with a grin. "I'm guessing you're from the United States, but I knew that even before you spoke."

The gondolier started talking loud enough for everyone to hear him, so Hannah didn't respond out of politeness. He began to describe the buildings they floated past, but Valentino pointed out others and whispered what they were in her ear.

"That building across the way is the best Italian restaurant in all of Italy, and over there, where it's all lit up, is where my father works," he told her. "And my brother lives in that villa up ahead on the left."

The boat docked twenty minutes later, and she was almost sad. She enjoyed Valentino's lively company. He was noticeably proud of his city.

"Thank you for the mini tour," she said after climbing onto the dock behind him. "Your city is beautiful."

He surprised her when he leaned in and planted a soft kiss on each cheek, murmuring, "Thank you for your company. It was my pleasure."

The only thing he hadn't pointed out was the mysterious man lurking in the shadows nearby, keeping a watchful eye on Hannah.

Five

Hannah took a cup of decaffeinated tea and a blanket out onto her balcony to look at the stars. She shivered when a breeze kicked up and tousled her hair, but then a bigger chill went down her spine when she saw a man standing under a lamp across the street. Even with the distance, she could tell that he was looking up at her.

She bustled back inside, locked the balcony door, and closed all the drapes. After five minutes, she peeked out the window and saw him still standing there. She couldn't see his face that well, but she could tell he was still looking up at her building.

She brushed her teeth and her hair before changing into her nightgown. Then she used a makeup removal towelette to clean her face. Before tucking herself in bed, she turned out the lights and peeked out the window once more. The man was still there.

Maybe he's a homeless man? Regardless of who he was, or what he was doing, she went to bed trembling enough to make her teeth chatter.

Hannah woke up at 5:30 Friday morning after a restless sleep. Before doing anything else, she jumped out of bed and looked out the window. The man was no longer there. Feeling relieved, but a little insecure, she put on her robe, fixed a cup of coffee, and went back out to the balcony to watch the sunrise.

After her coffee, she dressed in a green sweatshirt and white shorts. She pulled her hair into a ponytail and left her room to go for a jog down by the water.

She ran several blocks, enjoying the peaceful sound of the lapping water, before she turned around to go back.

"Ciao, Hannah!" Valentino's voice rang out from the sidewalk above, and he vigorously waved.

Hannah slowed down to a walk and waved back. "Ciao!" she called out to him. She stopped walking to wait for him while he took the stairs down to her.

"It's good to see you again," he commented with a broad grin.

"Thank you; although, I'm sure I'm a mess," she replied while using her sleeve to dab sweat from her forehead.

He waved her off. "Nah, sei molto bella. You're very beautiful."

Hannah felt a flood of warmth in her cheeks. "Grazie," she mumbled.

He smiled at her, and in the light of day, she noticed how nice it was. He had a slight indentation in his chin that was cute. He was an inch shorter than her, and he appeared close in age.

"I have to go to work now, but perhaps you'd like to join me for dinner at the restaurant I pointed out last night? I'm serious when I say they have the best food in all of Italy." He opened his arms in a wide gesture.

She chewed the inside of cheek. He seemed harmless, but still…Her mind flashed back to the creepy man watching her building last night. She knew it wasn't Valentino because that man appeared rather large in size.

"Please?" he asked. "I promise if you don't enjoy my company, you'll never see me again."

I have to eat, and it will be in public. "Okay," she relented. "I'll meet you there. What time?"

He bounced on his heels with a huge smile. "Is 6:00 too early?"

She shook her head. "I'll see you then. Enjoy your day at work."

"I will and thanks. Enjoy your day in Venice." He trotted back up the hill, taking the steps two at a time.

As she finished her trek back to the hotel, she felt excited about her date with the handsome Italian. She was going to take the opportunity to learn more about the beautiful country. While prancing up the steps, though, trepidation filled her when she felt the sensation of being watched.

She looked around, but she only saw a few people bustling down the busy street, and they weren't paying attention to her. She paid no mind to the black crow circling the sky.

Six

Hannah took a shower and ordered breakfast through room service. It was warming up outside, so she took her meal out onto the balcony. She watched the gondolas floating by while she ate, and she thought about her mini-tour with Valentino. She decided to take another ride after breakfast, so she could see all the buildings in the daylight.

Before leaving her hotel room, she went through her clothes to find the right outfit for her date. *A date? I've not been on a first date in over three years.* Excitement, curiosity, and a touch of anxiety tumbled together in her chest. She wondered if she'd be ready to put herself back on the market when she returned home. Her close friends had been on her case for months, trying to hook her up.

Her phone rang and halted her rummaging. It was her closest friend, Kristin. She glanced at her watch before answering; it was 8:30 in Italy which made it 2:30 a.m. in New York.

"Shouldn't you be in bed?" she greeted Kristin.

Her friend of several years laughed. "Who says I'm not? I couldn't sleep, and I knew you'd be up."

Hannah rolled her eyes. Her friend knew her well. "Yeah, well, I don't want to miss a minute of my vacation. I can sleep at home."

"And I can sleep when I'm dead," she retorted. "So, what's it like? Tell me everything!"

Hannah told her about the necklace and the other shopping. "Before you ask, no, I've not found your present yet, and I wouldn't tell you what it is anyway."

"Oh come on! You know I'm not a patient person," Kristin scoffed.

"Well, this will have to be an early gift then. I have a date tonight." She held the phone away from her ear because she knew what was coming.

"What?" Kristin shrieked. "*You* have a date? Are you yanking my chain?"

Hannah giggled. "No, I'm serious. I met an Italian guy on a gondola ride last night, and I ran into him this morning. He invited me to dinner."

"Oh? Where did you run into him? In your bed?"

Hannah's mouth fell open. "Uh! No. He spotted me when I was out jogging, and you know I'm not like that."

"Hmm, *anymore* you mean," she teased.

"Kristin Dawn Wright! You take that back, or I'm not bringing you back a present," Hannah warned.

Her friend laughed. "I take it back. It's about time you let go and have some fun, though."

"I'm sure I'll have a nice evening. Now, it's time for you to go back to sleep before you have to call in sick again," she chided.

They said a quick goodbye, and Hannah finished rummaging through her clothes. She chose a light-blue silk pant suit for her dinner date with Valentino. Then she left to go sight-seeing and shopping for the rest of the presents.

She went to a different dock and caught the first gondola ride. The buildings pointed out by the gondolier were different than the ones from the previous night. She was able to spot some that Valentino had indicated, including the restaurant he wanted to eat at. The man saw her straining to see the sign. She had to know where to tell the cab driver to go after all.

"That is the finest Italian restaurant in all of Venice. It's the Ristorante Alle Corone," he told her.

"Grazie," she replied and wrote it down on the notepad in her purse.

She got off at the next dock because she saw a Prada store. She still had to shop for Kristin and their friend Beth.

After browsing the store for thirty-five minutes, and wanting everything they had, she settled on a pair of sunglasses for each. That concluded her shopping for gifts, unless she wanted to get a couple of early birthday presents out of the way. She decided that she couldn't afford any more hits to her credit cards, though.

She stopped at a bistro on the walk back to the hotel and ordered a sandwich. While she ate and people watched, she noticed a black crow watching her from its perch on a nearby fence post. She tossed a small piece of bread its way, and it flew down to eat it. She tossed it more, which it continued to eat until one of the employees came out and shooed it away with a broom.

The man scowled at her. "Per favore non alimentare gli uccelli qui. Ti disturbano i clienti."

She frowned back at him and scrunched her brows together. She had no idea what he'd said.

"Excuse me," a woman eating nearby said. "You look confused, and I speak fluent Italian. He said, 'Please don't feed the birds here. They'll bother the customers.' "

"Oh, thank you," Hannah replied and then to the man, she apologized in Italian, "Mi dispiace."

"Meh," he chirped and shrugged before going back to his sweeping.

"Is this your first visit here?" the woman asked with a smile.

Hannah laughed and wiped the crumbs off her mouth. "Is it that obvious?"

The woman laughed now too. "I can usually spot newbies. My husband and I came here for the first time five years ago, and we fell completely in love with the culture. So, as soon as we got back home, we put the house on the market and moved here."

"That's incredible"—Hannah looked around the plaza—"I can see why, though."

The lady looked at her watch. "Oh! Speaking of my husband, I'm late in picking him up. It was nice chatting with you," she said while rising from her seat and hurrying away.

Hannah walked the mile back to the hotel since it was so nice out. She occasionally stopped to browse the shops along the way, but she didn't buy anything else.

In her hotel room, she locked the sunglasses inside the safe where she already had the other gifts. Then she took a glass of iced tea out to the balcony and watched the activity along the canal. A loud caw startled her, announcing that she wasn't alone. There was a black crow on the railing.

"I'm sorry, but I don't have any more food for you," she cooed to the bird, wondering if it was the same one from the bistro.

She used her phone to check her emails and voicemail. She had a message from her parents, who were wanting to know if she was having a nice trip. She quickly texted her mother that Italy was amazing.

It was 3:00, and she felt worn out after the long walk, so she decided to enjoy a nap. She put the "do not disturb" sign on the door and set her phone alarm for 4:30. That would give her plenty of time to clean up for her date.

Seven

At 5:45, Hannah hailed a taxi. She read the name of the restaurant off to the driver, who corrected her pronunciation with a knowing smile. He had her there promptly at 6:00. As soon as he pulled the car up to the entrance, she spotted Valentino—he was pacing nervously in front of the entrance.

"Grazie," she said as she handed the driver his cab fare. She climbed out and called out to Valentino.

"Good evening, Hannah!" he returned with a broad grin. "I hope you're hungry."

She felt more nervous than hungry, but of course, she wasn't going to tell him that. "Yes, I'm hungry," she said instead.

He opened the door for her, and the pleasant aroma of Italian cuisines washed over her and made her mouth water. She was hungry now.

"It smells good, si?" He asked and stopped at the hostess's podium.

"It smells delicious," she agreed.

After he provided his name, the hostess led them to an intimate table for two and gave them their menus.

"What do you recommend, Valentino?" she asked.

He looked up with a grin. "Please, call me Val, and I recommend everything. It's all magnifico."

Their server stopped off to get their drink orders, and they both decided on iced tea.

"I think I'm settling on the baked mostaccioli with meatballs," she announced.

"Excellent choice. I'm going to order my favorite, which is fettuccine alfredo."

The server returned with their teas and some garlic rolls, and then she took their orders.

When she was gone, Val asked, "So, how was your day in my beautiful city?"

She was chewing some of her roll, so she gave him a thumb up until she swallowed. "It was great. I ate at a bistro and got scolded for feeding a bird. I finished my shopping for souvenirs to take home to my loved ones, I took another gondola ride, and my run was good."

"Si, the pigeons are terrible around here," he moaned.

"Oh, it wasn't a pigeon; it was a crow." She took another bite of her roll just as the server returned with their salads.

He choked on his bread and made the Catholic sign over his chest while his face turned dark red. Just as she was about to dash over and pat him on the back to help him cough it up, he stopped. He took a deep breath and a drink to finish washing it down his throat.

"Whew! You really had me worried there," she commented. "I thought I was going to have to do the Heimlich maneuver on you."

He nodded. "Me too," he said in a hoarse voice. "You worried me when you said you fed a crow." He saw the look of confusion on her face, so he continued. "Italians are leery of crows. We believe they bring bad luck and are a foreboding of death."

She couldn't hold back the laughter that bubbled up. "I know that the Italian culture is full of superstitions, but a crow? A harmless bird? I didn't know that."

He narrowed his eyes at her and lowered his voice. "We are an old world. We know more than you think. Have you heard of the malocchio?"

"That's the evil eye, right?" she asked just as the server put her meal in front of her.

The server clutched a necklace she wore that looked like a chili pepper. "Beware the malocchio," she mumbled and bustled away.

Val noticed Hannah's amusement and repeated himself. "I told you, we are an old world. We know things."

The table grew silent while they dug into their meals. Then he talked about his family and asked about hers. They were so engrossed in conversation, that neither noticed the man staring in through the window.

The evening was pleasant with a warm breeze, so Val offered to walk her back to her hotel when they were finished with dinner. "Unless you'd prefer to take a taxi," he said.

"No. I think I need to walk after that heavy meal, or I won't sleep tonight. It was certainly delicious, though."

"Very well"—he offered his arm to her—"then I insist on escorting you safely."

She didn't feel comfortable taking his arm, so she pretended not to see the gesture. She was glad when he didn't say anything about it.

They walked a couple of blocks when the crowd of people thinned out. Except for a straggler here and there, it was just the two of them. A couple of the streetlamps had burned out bulbs, so shadows were everywhere. She heard footsteps coming from the dark and stepped closer to Val. She grabbed for his arm as a feeling of dread suddenly overcame her.

Val chuckled. "Don't be afraid," he whispered and squeezed her hand that was resting on his arm.

"I think I heard something," she whispered back.

He sighed and gave her another squeeze. "It's the city. She comes alive at night, but mostly it's harmless."

She blanched. "Mostly?"

"Well, yeah, you never know what could be lurking in the shadows. Crime rate is low here, but if you believe in the mysterious…"

"I don't believe in the mysterious," she quickly uttered in a tone that was meant to convince herself more than him. "I believe in what I can see and touch." She approached the steps that led up to her hotel. "Thank you for walking me back."

He shrugged. "It was my pleasure. Thank you for having dinner with me. I'd like to take you out again and soon. We can go dancing, or whatever you'd like to do."

She heard herself agree to his offer before she gave it serious thought. She had enjoyed his company both times, so why not? When in Rome…

"Magnifico! Can I have your phone number so I can arrange it?" He pulled his cell phone out and looked expectantly at her.

"Yes, of course." She rattled the numbers off to him and watched as he typed them in. Her phone then rang twice from her purse.

"There. Now you have mine. Call any time, and the sooner the better," he said with a wink.

"Thank you"—she looked up at the hotel—"I'd better get inside."

Before she could protest, he leaned in and kissed her on both cheeks, and then he kissed her on the lips. His mouth was soft and warm, and she let him move himself over her. His tongue slipped inside and played gently against hers until she gave in and kissed him back. It had been a long time, so she needed it.

Breaking it off, she told him again that she needed to go inside and get to bed. He grazed his fingertips over her cheek, brushing her hair aside.

"Good night then, beautiful lady," he murmured, gave her another soft kiss without tongue, and then sauntered away with a noticeable swagger in his step.

Her heart was fluttering like a million butterflies in her chest as she made her way up to the second floor and to her room. He was attractive and a good kisser. Plus, it had been months since she'd had physical contact with a man.

She washed up for bed and was just tucking herself in, wanting to relive the moment, when Kristin called.

"Sooo, how'd the date go? Don't you dare tell me you chickened out!" she greeted Hannah.

"Hello to you too, and it was nice. We went to dinner at a really good Italian restaurant, and then he walked me back to the hotel."

"Is he still there?" she whispered, and Hannah couldn't tell if she was teasing or being serious.

"No, he's not here. I let him kiss me good night, and then he left me at the steps to the hotel."

"Just a kiss? That's all?" Her disappointment was audible.

"That was enough," Hannah replied sternly. "I'm tired and off to bed. I'll tell you more tomorrow. Good night, Kristin."

"Okay, good night." The line went silent.

Feeling restless now, Hannah made a cup of decaf tea and went out to the balcony to enjoy the warm breeze. She quickly turned and went back inside, though, when she saw the man standing across the street and staring up at her again. This time, she called down to the lobby and reported it. She was placed on hold while the hotel security officer checked it out.

Several minutes later, he came back on the line. "Mademoiselle, I've checked all around the area and didn't see anyone. There's no one out there now, but I'll check again a little later to make sure he's still gone."

"Okay, thank you for looking," she mumbled.

"It's no problem. Buona sera, mademoiselle."

"Good night." She hung up the phone and crossed the room to peek outside. There was a black cat prowling around where the man had stood just moments ago. The bizarre thing about it, though, was it also looked up at her balcony.

Eight

Armand waited until the woman stepped inside before changing back. He'd seen the other man looking around just in time to shift into a cat. He was trying hard to adjust to the changes the world had made since he was entombed in 1610 by the one who wore the Jewel of Isis. Now, his sole purpose was to get close to its new keeper and destroy her, so he could then destroy it. She was the one who could help fulfill the prophecy, which would be his end for all eternity this time. The only problem he saw was the man who accompanied her twice now. He was the chosen one to protect her. He was from a long line of vampire hunters.

Armand looked up at the balcony again and sniffed the air. He could smell her sweet honeysuckle aroma from where he stood, and it beckoned him. The call of her blood was too strong to ignore. He'd already fed a few times, including on the man whose clothes he then donned to fit in with the times, but she made him hungry again.

He shifted into a crow, flew up to her balcony, and shifted back. She had left the balcony door unlocked, not that a lock would've been able to stop him. Like the silent roll of fog, he crept into her room. He could tell she was sound asleep because of her soft snores.

He made his approach and leaned over her. The nightgown she wore was filmy and hugged her feminine curves, creating another kind of longing inside him. Four hundred years was a long time to go without the feel of a woman. He grew hard while staring down at her, and he decided he needed to act upon it. The question was, did he feed first or relieve his physical lust first? He decided to do both at the same time.

In old-world Italian, he hypnotically chanted, "Si sono semplicemente sognando la mia bellezza. Non aprire gli occhi." *You are simply dreaming, my beauty. Do not open your eyes.*

He sat on the side of the bed, causing her to stir, but her eyes remained closed. He ran a hand over her sheathed body, admiring the feel of her and longing to see her naked just as much as he longed to taste her blood. He gave in to his pulsing and unlaced the ties on the bodice of her nightgown. He reached in and squeezed one soft breast and then the other, tracing the puckered buds with his long fingernail as he did so. She stirred and made a whimpering sound, but her eyes didn't open. He leaned in to take one rosy peak into his mouth and suckled, watching her brows knit together in sexual frustration as he applied more force. Her hands clawed at the bedding and then his shoulders when he used his teeth to nip her. He refrained from sinking his fangs into her soft flesh, though. Denying himself now would only make it sweeter when he gave in to his craving.

He ripped her gown open the rest of the way and ran his hand down her body to settle in her mound of soft dark curls. Her hips writhed on the bed when he began to pet her velvety smooth lips, and she bucked when he slipped a finger between them. He could smell the moisture collecting between her heavenly thighs, and it made the throbbing between his own more intense. He plunged a finger into her wetness, and the heat from her core almost made him burst. He opened the buttons on the pants he wore and let his rock-hard flesh spring free, which gave him some relief.

"Men of your time wear confining clothes, my beauty," he purred, and her brows furrowed again. He could tell she wanted to open her eyes, but alas, she was under his spell. "Soon, my beauty. I'll give you what you crave soon." He withdrew his finger from her heat and tasted her nectar. "Mmm, you're sweet, my lovely girl."

He shed the rest of his clothing and tossed them to the floor. Then he nudged her thighs apart to give them both what they needed. He put the head of his manhood at her entrance and prodded until her soft flesh yielded to him. A trickle of her juices made his movements easy as he filled her to the hilt, reaching the fiery depths of her core.

She bucked her hips against him, matching his rhythm, and filling the air around them with heavy panting and soft cries. Her hands clawed at his chest while he brought her enormous pleasure, so he took her wrists in one hand and pinned them above her head.

He looked down and saw a trickle of blood from her claw marks, and without any thought at all, he swiped it up with his free hand and stuck his finger into her mouth, wiping it against her soft tongue. It was the only way to turn a human into a vampire, but it had to be done three times, with the final time occurring during a full moon. He hadn't intended to create a mate, so his gesture surprised him. Even hundreds of years ago, when he roamed the earth, he didn't have a female companion; although, he'd enjoyed female company often. He'd just always left them satisfied but drained.

He continued to pump her body until his lust finally burst inside her. While he climaxed, he lifted her left breast and sank his teeth into the underside. Her red nectar spilled into his starving mouth and caused a warming sensation to fill his belly while her keening noise filled his ears. He suckled enough to satiate his appetite without taking her life. He couldn't kill her even though that was his original intent. She simply tasted too perfect. He used his saliva to close the puncture marks up, leaving only a hint of red left. That would fade within a day, though. It helped vampires to go undetected.

He redressed and left through the balcony doors. Once he was gone, his slumber spell would soon wear off. He would be back soon, though. He was certain of it.

Nine

Hannah's eyes felt so heavy as she tried to open them Saturday morning. Someone was shouting at her, but she couldn't comprehend at first.

"Housekeeping!" the voice repeated.

Housekeeping? It's too early. She glanced at her phone display; it was already 11:00. She quickly sat up in the bed, but her head was pounding so hard that she fell back onto the pillow.

"Come back later, please," she called out in a hoarse voice.

"Si. Grazie," the woman replied.

Hannah looked at the time again and squinted her eyes at the sunlight streaming in through her window. She never slept in past 7:00—if she didn't wake up on her own by then, her dog made sure to get her up. She missed Sam, her German Shephard. She'd never been away from him overnight in the two years she'd had him, so she was certain he was missing her too.

She forced herself out of bed and found some aspirin in her purse. It hurt to swallow. It hurt to think. She looked down, when she felt a draught, and found her nightgown ripped open. *Whoa. What the hell happened here?*

She removed what was left of the garment and climbed into a hot shower, hoping it would help ease her headache and wake her up. When she washed, she noticed that her breast hurt, and she noticed a soreness between her legs too. Then she remembered a dream she'd had. It was a hot and heavy sex dream that made her turned on just to think about it. The room had been black, but she had heard his velvety, seductive voice as he urged her to yield to him. Then he gave her agonizing pleasure as he filled her body with his hard heat. Of course, a dream didn't explain her tenderness now. It didn't explain her shredded nightgown either.

Hanna had lucid dreams on occasion, but it was never like that one. That sex dream was beyond amazing. It must've been Val seducing her, she thought, and it made her want to see him again. Maybe there was something to him after all. Maybe she was denying herself when she should take Kristin's advice.

Her phone beeped, bringing her out of her reverie. She had a text from Val.

Good morning, beautiful lady. How is your day so far? I was hoping to see you jogging again, but alas, I'm left denied of your captivating presence. I have a surprise for you this afternoon if you're up to it. Would you meet me at the main gondola dock at 2:00?

She texted back that she would, and excitement filled her as she went through her clothes to pick out something for whatever he had planned. She decided on a lavender tennis skirt, white top, and her new sandals from Gucci.

It was 12:00, so she ordered up a salad for lunch. She didn't want to eat too much in case he was thinking of having a bite with her. *Bite? Did he bite me in my dream?* That detail was hazy, but she thought she could recall being bitten, and the thought made her tingle.

After lunch in her room, she went out onto the balcony for some fresh air. She smelled something musky, but she couldn't tell where it was coming from. She looked across the street, but no one was there. She looked at the balconies above and below, but they were also vacant. Regardless of where it came from, she liked the fragrance. It smelled *masculine*.

She heard flapping and watched a black crow land on the railing again. "Shoo," she told the bird, but it didn't budge. She got closer and waved it away, but again, it stayed put.

"Damn superstitions," she mumbled to herself.

The bird cocked its head and didn't display any fear of her whatsoever. It was mocking her. She was starting to see why Italians feared them.

Her phone chimed, beckoning her back inside. It was a new text from Val.

I got off work early. Can you meet me in 30 minutes?

She answered that she could, and then she rushed to change her clothes, freshen her makeup, and catch a cab.

Val was waiting for her at the dock when she arrived, and he was the only person there.

"Where is the gondolier?" Hannah inquired while looking all around.

"Right here," he answered and gestured to himself.

Her brow shot up, and she wore an amused grin. "You're joking, right?"

He shook his head, though. "I would never tease you. I rented the boat for the afternoon because I want to show you Italy in my own way."

She smirked at him. "Do you know how to drive one of these things?"

"Si. This isn't my first time." He wore a cocky grin and gestured for her to get into the boat.

I bet it isn't. "So, then how many American women have you floated up and down the canal?" She asked while taking a seat in the front, so they could talk.

He laughed while picking up the large pole used for steering the vessel. "Are you asking how many notches I have on my *pole*?"

"So to speak," she answered with a roll of her blue eyes.

"Oh, well, my guess would be in the upper hundreds, and not just women. There have been men too." He pushed the gondola away from the dock, and she admired his bulging biceps.

"Huh?"

He erupted in laughter. "I used to work as a gondolier. It was my job for almost two years."

She nodded in understanding. That was much better than what she had imagined. She looked around at the scenery, absorbing as much of it as she could before she had to go back home to reality.

"Are you feeling all right today?" he suddenly asked, making her jump.

"Well, I had fitful dreams last night and ended up oversleeping this morning, so I'm not sure. I may be coming down with something. I still feel tired."

He studied her with intensity. "You look a little pale; so maybe you are coming down with something."

"I think I'm hallucinating too. There was a crow on my balcony, and it wouldn't go away," she mentioned.

He mumbled something under his breath in either Italian or another language she wasn't familiar with. "What are you saying?" she wondered.

He opened his mouth to reply, but he snapped it shut, forced a smile, and told her, "It's nothing. Don't worry about it." What he'd said in Arabic was, "The dead are here. They are walking among us."

The dead was closer than he knew. It was circling the sky right above them.

He stopped pushing with the pole and sat down next to her, letting the current float them along. He put one arm around her waist and gave her a squeeze while pointing at lush rolling hills.

"My parents live on that hillside," he professed.

She looked at him out of the corner of her eye and smirked. "Hmm, I don't see it. It must be a small house."

He bumped his shoulder against hers but laughed in the process. When a warm breeze tousled her hair against her cheek, he brushed it away and leaned in for a kiss. With minimal hesitation, she accepted his mouth and let him plunder her hot depths with his soft tongue. His kiss was soft and yielding, while his hands on her waist were firm as he squeezed her hips. He ran one hand up her back and through her hair, which she loved. His kisses quickly grew heady, and she could hear them both panting.

"Stop," she said as she pulled away. Then she forced herself to look into his warm brown eyes, so she could explain. "I can't. I'm leaving soon."

He tilted his head to the left. "I know, and that's why we need to enjoy every second we can. It will have to hold us over until you can come back, or I can come there."

Her eyes widened. "Look, I don't have anyone at home, and I'm keeping it that way for now. I can't do a local relationship, much less a long distance one. I'm sorry if you thought this could turn into something."

She was surprised when he gave her a relaxed grin. "I'm not that easy to get rid of, and I think you'll come around."

"What makes you think that?" she inquired with a squint.

"I come from psychics, remember?" he told her in a quirky voice. He rose and used the stick to push them a little farther up the canal. "Actually, I also come from Egyptians, and I wanted to speak to you about that."

Ten

The crow swooped in as close as it could without being noticed by the man. It listened in and caught him mention Egypt. That only proved Armand's earlier suspicion that the man was part of another generation of vampire hunters. He had to find a way to kill the man before he could run off with the beautiful lady; otherwise, the hunter would just keep coming after him and her, too, once she was turned. That is if he completed her transformation. It would be up to him to repopulate the world with vampires, so why not create a beautiful one to use for his pleasure? He had time to think about it because the moon wouldn't be full for a few days yet.

Armand figured it was at least five hours until sundown, so all he could do for now was follow the couple and try to overhear what they talked about.

The smell of honeysuckle was carried to him on a breeze, and his little bird heart beat faster. He would take her body again before he took her blood, and then he would feed her more of his.

He overheard her name, and it played repeatedly through his mind. *Darling Hannah, either way I'm going to kill you. So sorry.* It was the nature of the beast. It was survival of the fittest. First, of course, he needed to dispatch her warrior, and the sooner the better.

He watched them carefully as they docked, and the man helped her from the boat. He didn't like the hunter's hands on his prey. He flew close enough to overhear them.

"Thank you, Val. I had a nice time. I'm sorry I'm not feeling well. I didn't even give you a chance to tell me about Egypt," she said.

"I will tell you all about it soon. In fact, I'd like to check on you this evening. I'll drop by your hotel to make sure you're okay," he offered. "I might even bring you chicken soup," he added with a wink.

She laughed at his suggestion. "I suppose that will be fine unless I'm feeling worse. Please call or text before you make the trip."

"Of course. Now, are you sure you don't want me to walk you back?" He reached out and took her left hand in his right.

"Yes, I'm sure. You have things to do, and I'm all right. I'm just exhausted," she assured him.

"Hopefully, I didn't bore you today," he said and leaned in to kiss her.

Hannah pulled away from Val to avoid his advance. "I might have something contagious. I'll talk to you later." She turned and walked away before she let herself lose control and acted out her dream.

The crow's wings fluttered to let the warrior know it was watching. The man responded by backing away and then hurrying down the sidewalk.

Eleven

The crow followed Hannah back to her hotel and then flew up to her balcony when she went inside. She had the curtains open, so it perched to where it could watch her. All it needed to do was wait for nightfall, and while it waited, it planned.

Armand hated not being able to touch her when she undressed and slipped into bed. Since he'd ruined her nightgown, she slept in her white bra and panties. Her exposed flesh made him ache to kiss it, to lick it, and to drink from it. She tossed and turned, kicked the cover off, pulled it back on, and finally got up and paced the confines of her room.

She felt out of sorts. She looked down at her hands, and they were trembling. She hadn't had too much caffeine, so an explanation, like sleep, eluded her. She put her robe on, so she could step out onto the balcony. When she reached for the door handle though, she saw something that added to her agitation—the crow. It sat on the small table and focused its beady black eyes on her, staring her down. She wished Valentino had never mentioned his superstitions.

She let go of the door handle and lay back down. She thrashed the covers and pillows, trying to get comfortable, but it didn't work. Her body was undeniably exhausted, but her mind was restless.

Her phone chimed from its spot on the nightstand, so she picked it up. It was a text from Val.

I know it hasn't been long, but I'm concerned about you. I'm in your lobby, and I have something for you. Can I come up?

She couldn't stop herself from smiling as she typed back her room number. She quickly dressed and picked up her dirty laundry from the floor. Just as the evidence of her sloppiness was stashed out of sight, there was a knock on her door.

"Room service!" he called out with a heavy French accent.

She opened the door, telling him with a fake accent of her own, "It's about time. I ordered that days ago." It turned out, he did have food. He had a bowl of chicken noodle soup for her. "Yum! That smells delicious, but you didn't have to go out and get that for me. I'll be fine."

"I *made* it for you because I wanted to. It's my mother's recipe, and it has always made me feel better." He looked through the balcony door and gestured with his head. "Would you like to sit outside? It's still nice out."

Hannah hesitated at first, but then she wanted to see his reaction to the bird out of morbid curiosity. "Sure."

He opened the door for her, and she stepped through while looking left and right for the crow; however, it was nowhere to be seen. *Odd.*

"I bet you come out here frequently. The view is wonderful," he exclaimed and gestured toward the canal.

"Yes, I've sat out here a few times until..." She didn't know how much she wanted to reveal to him.

"Until what?" he pressed.

She took a deep breath and pointed across the street to the lamppost where the creepy man had stood watching her balcony twice so far. "Until a shady looking fellow drove me back inside."

His face became ashen. "Explain," he commanded in a stern voice that surprised her.

She laughed nervously at herself. "I feel foolish for talking about this. It's just that he was staring up at me. At least I think he was; it was dark both times, so I guess I could be wrong."

Val ran his hands through his hair and sighed. "I don't think you were wrong."

Her heart rate increased just from his tone, but the implication of his words made her head spin. She swallowed hard and choked out, "What are you saying?"

His jaw was clenched when he sighed, "I think you are in danger."

Her blood left her face. She looked at him with panic in her eyes, and worry lines etched her forehead. "Why would I be in danger?" Her voice, which was barely above a whisper, cracked with emotion. "And from whom?"

He sat down across from her at the small table and stared at the soup she hadn't touched yet. He cleared his throat and began to tell her of his heritage.

"Let me tell you about my family history before I answer that because it's all entwined together. My father's family is from Egypt, while my mother's family is from Italy. I was born and raised here, but I learned about my father's side of the family when I was quite young. It's actually something I've not thought about until I met you.

"My father's ancestors were vampire hunters in Egypt, and it has always been in my blood, but I've never had to pay attention to it until now. Until I met you."

She held one hand up to stop him. "Just a second. What…what the hell are you talking about? There is no such thing as vampires. I mean, I suppose there are people who *think* they are vampires, and maybe they drink blood, but actual living-dead vampires? No. I don't buy that shit."

His expression was serious and never wavered. She could tell he believed the words he was spewing, but that didn't mean she had to. The man on the street corner was just a man. Perhaps he was admiring the building. For all she knew, he could be an architect. He certainly wasn't a vampire.

Val looked away toward the setting sun. "I promise you that they are real," he stated with emotion pouring out.

"Well, why haven't I ever heard of them being real then? How come they are just monsters in movies where I come from?"

He met her wide-eyed stare. "Because of two reasons. For one thing, we keep to ourselves here. It's our culture and our burden to deal with. Secondly, they were destroyed when the Jewel of Isis was made by mankind in homage to the Egyptian goddess, who offered her protection from the immortals."

She cleared her throat to interrupt him. "I've heard that story, I think. But if they were destroyed, then why would you be worried about it now? Not that I'm saying I buy into this."

He gave her a look that said his patience was wearing thin with her. "I have no reason to lie to you. I'm not making up a tall tale to impress you." His voice was gruff like a father's when scolding his child.

She was sure her cheeks were red from the reprimanding. "Go on then. I'm listening." She decided to hear him out fully before recommending mental health assistance.

"It was believed back then that the strongest of the blood-hungry creatures were entombed as opposed to being destroyed. They survived Isis's wrath, but the threat was still removed."

Hannah bit her lip while she digested the theory. "How can they be released from entombment?"

"I need to seek my father's council to answer that since he is more knowledgeable about the matter. You should come with me to talk to him." He tapped his fingertips on the table, and she wanted to reach out and slap his hand so he'd quit.

"That's another question I have. What do I have to do with all of this? Why would a vampire be after *me*? Furthermore, how would you know about it if one was?"

He gave her a half-smile, but the lines in his forehead told her he wasn't teasing. "I told you the night we met that I'm from a line of psychics, which is on my mother's side. I just feel a negative energy around you, and it makes me feel like I need to protect you. As for why, I don't know. That's also something I want my father to explain to us. Will you come with me?"

Hannah felt dizzy and gripped the table to keep herself steady. "I don't know. I need some time to think about what you're saying."

He stood up and pointed a finger at her and then at the setting sun. "You may not have much time to think about it. Now is the time to act."

She slapped her palm on the table causing shards of pain to shoot up her arm. "What? What the fuck do you want me to say? That I believe in this shit? Well, I don't. I think you're just trying to scare the tourist. It's probably some sick game you get off on."

He looked pained. "I assure you it's not. I'm not making anything up." His voice was soft and meant to be comforting, but she didn't feel soothed by it.

She covered her face with her hands. *This is a bad dream. It's just a bad dream, and I'm going to wake up now.* She pulled her hands away, and of course Val was still there, watching the skyline.

"I can't talk about this anymore today. If you want me to meet your father, it will have to wait until tomorrow. I think you should go now." She rose from the table and headed indoors.

"No, I'm not leaving you. I'm going to stay and keep watch," he announced.

She spun around to face him. "And what would you do if one showed up? How would you fight it?"

He opened his mouth to speak, but nothing came out.

"That's what I thought. See? You don't need to stay with me because you don't even know what to do. Please go." She gestured toward the door.

"I wish you'd reconsider," he said and made no attempt to leave.

"I won't, and I'd like to go to bed. I didn't sleep earlier."

"All right, but tomorrow, we find answers. Do you agree?"

She nodded with a scowl. "Fine. I'll go with you tomorrow like I said. Good night."

After she closed and locked the door behind him, she wondered if sending him away was the right thing to do.

Twelve

Hannah paced the room, trying to make sense of the story Val spun. It just wasn't possible. How could it be?

She turned on the television to quiet her mind, but almost everything was in Italian. Then she found the local news, which had English subtitles, and tuned in. The reporter talked about several recent murders in Venice. The local police had no suspects, but they believed it was the same perpetrator because all four victims had broken necks.

"I'm pretty sure vampires don't break necks," she muttered to herself and turned off the TV.

She noticed it was dark outside, and she was tempted to look at the corner across the street to see if the man was standing there. However, she knew she wouldn't be able to fall asleep if she saw him, so she refrained and got ready for bed.

After her conversation with Val, she didn't want to fall asleep in the dark. She opened the curtain to allow the warm glow from the streetlamp to stream in, and while she hadn't needed a nightlight since she was little, she found it comforting. The fact that the man wasn't standing out there was even more comforting. If he had been, she would've immediately called Val and asked him to come back over.

Exhaustion finally settled in, and she fell asleep within a few minutes of climbing into bed. She started to dream about Val. They were on the gondola, with no one else around, and he held her close to kiss her. It wasn't long before his hands began to roam over her body, heightening her desire for him to keep going until he explored every inch of her.

Armand waited on the balcony for her to fall asleep. If she'd opened that curtain too, she would've seen him. The door was locked this time, so he used his telekinetic powers to flip the latch. With undetected movement, he slid the door open and stepped inside.

She must have been hot because she was sleeping in the nude, and her blanket was pushed aside. He used his exceptional night vision to drink in the lovely sight, and his body was quick to respond. While his erection painfully throbbed, his mouth salivated at the aroma of sweet honeysuckle.

Since he didn't want her to wake up, he whispered sensually, "Rimanete addormentati e godetevi i vostri sogni, bellissimi." *Stay asleep and enjoy your dreams, beautiful one.*

He sat on the edge of her bed and admired her radiance. He was mesmerized by the flush in her cheeks— it was the sign of a beating heart. Her full, pink lips beckoned him. He leaned in to kiss her this time, and her lips were warm and welcoming. She openly accepted his tongue and worked her own against it. The blistering kiss made his longing for her grow stronger, and it pulsated through his stiff tumescence. He opened his pants to give himself some relief.

Kissing her filled him with fire where he once had a soul, and he could hold back no more. He trailed his mouth across her cheek to the length of her lovely neck, pausing over her strong pulse. It would be so easy to tear into the vein and take what he needed, but he wanted all of her, so he held his hunger back.

He shed his pants and bore into her body, not wasting time with foreplay, and he found her already wet for him. He had to push a few times to get himself fully inside her, and it was agony of the sweetest kind. He flexed his hips with long strokes, reveling in the fact that the dark juices of her flesh would soon be his. For now, though, he enjoyed the sensation of her other juices as they coated the length of him.

She let out cries of surrender while he brought her to pleasure several times. Her face tightened each time before she shattered around him, and it made her more beautiful in his smoldering crimson eyes.

He took one rosy tip into his starving mouth and suckled. Her writhing beneath him became frenzied while he worked it with his lips and tongue. Her rapidly beating heart was loud to his ears, and her blood sang to him like no other sound on earth. He couldn't hold his thirst back any longer. His fangs sank into the softness of her breast, drawing her hot blood onto his tongue. It tasted incredibly sweet, unlike the usual saltiness he tolerated, and it appeased his palate like no other. His eyes rolled back as he fed with long pulls, and he had to fight his hunger to make himself stop, lest he bring death upon her.

He licked his lips clean and closed his eyes to concentrate on pleasuring her. Her body clenched him again, and it brought about his own release with a growl. His seed flooded her while he bit into his wrist to draw just enough of his blood.

She accepted the crimson fluid, but it wasn't of her own will. She licked her lips clean when he withdrew from her mouth and body. He could tell she was trying to open her eyes, but she was still enchanted by the incantation.

He leaned in and lapped at the bite mark on her breast. It closed, leaving just two tiny red blemishes. He didn't refrain from plundering her mouth again, tasting her sweet life while she still clung to it. Just one more taste of his blood, underneath the coming full moon, and she'd be his immortal bride. He had no idea if there were others of his kind roaming around, so her companionship might be welcomed. However, he still hadn't made up his mind about that yet. Even when he was mortal, he hadn't chosen a woman to spend his life with.

He put his pants back on and fled into the blackness of the night. He still needed to feed, and this time, he wouldn't stop until his prey's heart stopped.

Hannah clung to her erotic dream about Val as long as she could, but then her eyes flew open. She inhaled deeply, picking up an enticing musky fragrance, and her hand flew to her tender breast. It was strangely sore where Val had bit her in her dream.

She got up to use the bathroom and wobbled. The room was spinning, so she plopped back onto the bed until her head cleared. Her hand flew to her face to check for a fever, but she was cool to the touch. When the room stopped moving and her stomach settled, she slowly rose and made her way to the bathroom.

When she washed her hands, she glanced at the mirror, and that's when she noticed the red marks on her breast. She touched the sore area and wondered if she'd been bitten by a spider. "Or a vampire," she mused aloud. "Nah, there'd be visible holes if a vampire bit me."

She went back to bed and noticed the wet spot on the sheet for the first time. *Damn. Now, that's what you call a wet dream.* She had no trouble falling back to sleep, where Val met her again in the dream realm for another round of seduction.

Thirteen

Sunday morning began at 11:00 with wooziness and another pounding headache for Hannah. She took three aspirin and a hot, relaxing shower once the room stopped spinning. The red marks she'd seen on her bosom the night before were less visible now. Brushing it off, still thinking it might have been a spider bite, she went about drying her hair and applying a light layer of makeup.

She ordered a late breakfast from room service and took a cup of coffee out onto the balcony. The day was overcast with a low rumble of thunder in the distance, telling her she wouldn't do much sightseeing or shopping unless she bought an umbrella first.

The rain breeze felt good as it tousled her long hair, and she inhaled deep, relaxing breaths to help finish off the last of her headache. She could smell bread baking, and it made her mouth water just as there was a knock on her door.

"Room service," a voice called out, and it reminded her of Val when he'd brought her soup. She never did eat it either; it was still sitting on the small table inside the room.

She accepted her tray of bacon and eggs with whole wheat toast and went back outside. The thunder was sounding closer, but she figured she had a few minutes yet before the first raindrops fell.

Another sound, which was much closer, caught her attention. It was a scratching noise coming from her left. Ivy vines climbing the building were shaking, and then a black cat suddenly popped onto her balcony.

"Oh!" she exclaimed with a jump. "You startled me."

The cat rubbed against her bare leg, meowing for her attention. She handed it some of her toast, which it gobbled in one bite, causing the tip of its fangs to pierce her finger.

"Ouch! You don't have to bite, fella. I'll give you more," she exclaimed.

Her finger was bleeding from the nip, so she wiped it off on her napkin before handing more toast and a piece of bacon to the cat. It happily purred as it consumed the small feast.

It began to sprinkle as lightning creased the sky overhead. "Well, I guess I'd better go inside, and I don't know how you're going to get back down, so come on."

She grabbed her dishes and slid the door open. The cat scampered in before her and ran to her bed, where it jumped up and made itself comfortable on her pillow.

"Okay, make yourself at home," she mused and fetched a towel to dry herself off. Then she used the towel on the cat, hoping that housekeeping wouldn't say anything about the fur that clung to it. "You know, pets aren't allowed here, so you can't stay. But, I suppose you can't go out in this storm"—she looked out the balcony door at the downpour—"so you're stuck with me for a little while at least." The loud purring told her the cat was quite content with the arrangement.

She hung the "do not disturb" sign on the door, to buy herself some time, and climbed into the bed with the feline. She used the remote to turn on the television to the news channel where another gruesome murder was reported. This victim also had a broken neck. The reporter stated that police were requesting all citizens and tourists to abide by a 9:00 curfew and travel in pairs or groups. It was believed that all the murders had occurred at night, so restaurants, pubs, shops, and tourist attractions would be closing by the imposed curfew until the killer was caught.

Hannah stroked the cat's back while chills coursed through her. "Maybe Val should be worried about this guy instead of vampires," she mumbled under her breath. "What do you think, kitty?" The cat rubbed up against her in response.

Her cell phone rang and made her jump in surprise. She flipped it over and saw Val's name displayed, and her stomach fluttered as she recalled the erotic dreams she'd had about him.

"Hi, Val. I'm fine if that's why you're calling," she answered.

He laughed softly. "While I did want to check up on you, I also wanted to let you know that I'll be over in about twenty minutes to pick you up. If you recall, you said you'd meet my dad."

She sighed and stroked the cat with her free hand. "I remember," she mumbled.

"Great. So, I'll be there in twenty. Bye," he chirped and hung up.

Hannah pet the cat for a couple more minutes before getting up to check her hair and makeup. She decided to put her hair up in a simple ponytail for the day, tying a sheer pink scarf around it for some style. She changed her sweatpants out for a pair of pink shorts and put on her tennis shoes since it was raining, and she didn't want to ruin her leather sandals. She hoped he was bringing an umbrella.

"Okay, kitty, I can't leave you here without a litter box, so you're going to have to go when I do."

The sudden knock on her door startled her. She looked at her watch and noticed he was about five minutes early. She opened and found him hiding behind a bouquet of vibrant pink lilies.

"Those are beautiful. Thank you," she gushed.

He smiled and stepped into the room behind her while she went to the table to set the vase down. "They are lovely, but they're not as lovely as you."

She laughed. "I bet you say that to all the American girls," she teased. I see they are watered, which reminds me. Did you bring an umbrella?"

He opened his arms wide. "A giant one."

"Good. I don't think I'd melt, but I'd rather not tempt the fates." She looked around the room, realizing she didn't see the cat. "Come here, kitty. Come out, come out wherever you are," she cooed.

Val raised a brow at her. "Kitty? Did you get a pet while here?"

She waved him off and walked into the bathroom. The cat wasn't there, though. She called out to it again, and it finally meowed and came out from its hiding spot under the bed.

"There you are. Why are you hiding?" she asked.

The cat narrowed its eyes at Val and hissed, baring its claws and fangs. Val didn't seem to like it either because he jumped backward before the cat reacted to him.

"What's with you two?" Hannah asked.

Val's face paled. "Well, I don't know about him, but it's bad luck to have a black cat cross your path. Surely, you've heard that before."

Hannah grunted, "Lord, not with the superstitions again. Do you have one about everything?" She picked the cat up and cuddled it to her chest.

He cocked his head at her, and amusement danced in his eyes. "What's that you said earlier about not tempting the fates?" Then his expression changed, and his mouth formed a tight line. "Also, there's a connection between animals and the you-know-what."

She mouthed his words back to him. "I think you can say the word vampire aloud. It's a cat, not the CIA."

He looked at his feet. "Where did the cat come from? I mean, why do you have it?"

She scratched the animal between its ears as it nuzzled against her neck. "He climbed up the ivy vines and popped onto my balcony this morning."

He pointed at it. "And between that and the crow, you don't see anything strange? Let's go talk to my father; you need a wake-up call. He's expecting us anyway."

She hesitated. She didn't want everything she knew about life and the world to be turned upside down because of European superstitions and folklore. However, she had promised to go with him to hear the man out, and she was never one to go back on her word. Who knew? Maybe his father would actually side with her and tell Val to drop it.

"All right, I'm ready. I need to drop this little fella off outside along the way." She grabbed her purse and room key, following Val to the door. She took the sign off first, and then they made their way to the stairs.

They were able to sneak the cat out unnoticed by the hotel staff and other patrons. She set it down under the awning and gently patted it on its behind.

"All right, fella. This is where we part ways. Go on home now," she cooed, and the cat scurried through the rain and into some nearby shrubs.

"This way," Val said and nodded his head to his left. "I parked over there."

Hannah felt her nerves jumping all over the place. Not only was she getting into a car with a man she barely knew in another country, but she was headed someplace where all her beliefs might be shattered.

Fourteen

Hannah stared out the passenger side window at the bleak sky. The day was an ugly shade of gray.

"Did you hear about the curfew?" she suddenly asked.

His mouth was in a tight line. "Yes, and I'm glad the police are enforcing it. No one else should have to die."

She narrowed her eyes at him. "You don't think that that's related to…" She felt foolish and didn't want to complete her sentence.

"I'm not sure. I want to wait and see what my father says about it," he replied in a solemn tone.

"But they died from broken necks." She fiddled with her purse strap, trying to distract herself from the dread that filled her chest.

He simply shrugged and then pulled into a long driveway. At the end, sat a charming yellow house. Hannah looked around to see how close neighbors were in case this was a bad idea. Her mother would certainly scold her for going home with a complete stranger—especially one in a foreign land.

"We're here," he stated the obvious. "Let's go get you some answers."

With a trembling hand, she opened the passenger door and followed him up the walkway.

A large man with dark hair and a golden complexion opened the front door before Val could.

"Valentino, come on in. There's much to discuss," he proclaimed in a thick accent that wasn't Italian.

Val tugged on her hand, and they followed him inside. "Father, this is Hannah."

The man turned to face her and smiled with a mouthful of crooked teeth. "Hello, Hannah. I'm Alim

Aleron. Please have a seat so we can talk about what's going on out there." He nodded toward the window. "I understand that my son has many questions, and they are centered around you."

She sat down on the edge of the sofa with Val to her right, and a small dark-haired woman entered the room with a tray full of colas.

"Hello and welcome to our home. I'm Anna, Val's mother."

"Hello and grazie. Your home is lovely," Hannah replied and accepted a can of cola from her.

"Grazie," she replied and took a seat across from her husband.

"So, my son tells me that he believes the dead are walking among us, and that they are connected to you," Alim began.

Wow. Straight to the point.

"He also tells me that you don't share the beliefs of our people, and I can understand that. We aren't gathered here now to force something down your throat, but if you are indeed in danger, then it involves us, and we cannot ignore that. I can already see by your expression that you have many questions." He took a sip of his cola while he waited on her response.

Hannah bit her bottom lip. "Well, I don't understand *why* you believe in vampires. If they really existed outside of movies, wouldn't we know about them in the US?"

He nodded in understanding while she spoke and then replied, "Your culture used to believe many years ago when the Pilgrims reached the Americas. I'm sure you've heard of the witch trials, right? Well, that was part of it. Some of the people accused of witchcraft were actually vampires. But, over time, people became less believing. Evil was classified as acts of Satan instead of witches, vampires, werewolves, and so on. It might also be because most vampires stayed around Europe. They didn't have the means to travel, undiscovered, to the Americas. And, as I believe my son has explained, hundreds of years ago, Isis blessed a jewel that destroyed them. Well…all but the strongest which were entombed; although, we don't know where."

"Yes, he told me, and I heard the story elsewhere too. I asked Val how come he believed the vampires were back and why they would be after me, but he said you'd have to tell me."

Alim got out of his seat and crossed the room to a bookcase where he retrieved a book that looked to be at least one hundred years old. He opened it to the middle and then flipped a couple of pages before showing her what he was looking for.

"Have you seen this before?" he questioned.

She and Val both looked at the photo of a brilliant red gem, and she instantly recognized it. Fear clutched her heart in an icy grip as realization crept over her. "Yes, I've seen it. That's the Jewel of Isis, right? It's a necklace now." *And that's why a vampire is after me—because I have it.*

"Yes. It's kept safe in our Accademia Museum," he replied.

On a hoarse whisper, she informed them, "Not anymore."

"What do you mean?" he and Val asked in unison.

Her body was trembling, which made it difficult to answer. She looked down at her lap, took a deep breath, and mumbled, "I have the necklace."

"You do?" Val shrieked, and she saw a mixture of shock and concern in his chocolate drop eyes. "How? Did you steal it?"

Her head snapped back. "I did not! I'm a curator for the Metropolitan Museum of Art in New York. I acquired it on behalf of the museum." She swallowed loudly, knowing what they were going to say before the words were voiced.

Her suspicions were quickly confirmed. "That's what the vampire is seeking." Alim announced, "And that's why Val could sense the danger surrounding you."

Hannah stood and paced the living room. "But how would a vampire know that I have the necklace, and why wasn't it looking for it before? And how could the vampire be released from entombment anyway?"

"Father?" Val interjected.

Alim put the book back on the shelf and clasped his hand on her shoulder. "Because there is a second part to the story, which Val doesn't even know."

Wooziness overcame her, so she shrugged out of his clasp and went back to her seat on the couch. "What is that?" she squeaked out in a voice she didn't recognize.

He focused his piercing black eyes on her. "It was prophesied that one day, the earth would move and wake a powerful sleeping vampire. The vampire would then seek the Jewel of Isis to destroy it, allowing the creature to roam for eternity. The world would rest in the hands of a powerful warrior, who would destroy the creature and any others it woke up or created." He looked at his son with pride in his smile. "I just never knew that the warrior would be my son."

She blanched. "How do you know it's Val? Why couldn't it be talking about you?" Out of the corner of her eye, she saw Val grimace.

"I know that it's him because I didn't feel the disturbance in the energy around us until he brought it to my attention. He felt the shift first."

Shift…The earth would move. "Is this because of the earthquake that just happened? I thought you had them all the time." She stared at him, pleading with her eyes for him to make sense of everything.

"Indeed, we have several, but never with an avalanche following thereafter. I think that had something to do with it," Alim answered somberly.

She pointed to Val and commented, "And how is he a *powerful* warrior? I don't see how he could protect me."

Alim looked lovingly at his son before answering her. "He will have the strength and skills he needs, and he'll have me there to back him up if he needs me. His power comes from his ancestry; he was born with it."

She looked at Anna, who had been quiet the entire time. "Do you believe all of this too?"

She nodded with a smile and spoke softly. "Si. I have known of the legend since I met my Alim. His ancestry is full of powerful vampire hunters."

Hannah narrowed her eyes at the woman. "And it doesn't bother you that they want to do what they…do?"

"Oh, not at all. They have a higher calling, and it makes me proud."

"Aren't you worried, though?" Hannah shifted on the couch and recrossed her legs.

Val's mother nodded slowly this time, and her smile faded. "Si, but they can't deny their destiny. It's out of my hands." She opened her hands up with a shrug.

"I'll be fine. I was born for this like my father and his father before him," Val stated. "And I've already started training."

She jerked her head to the side to look at him. "What exactly does that mean? What kind of training?"

He smiled with boyish charm, and it reminded her of a kid at Christmas. "I've been practicing self-defense moves, and I've been looking through the diaries of my ancestors to see the best methods for battle and for destroying the blood suckers."

She spun around to look at his father. "That reminds me. The news hasn't reported anything about vampires. There's a serial killer out there breaking necks, though. Why would a vampire break necks, or is that someone else? And why, if it is a vampire, wouldn't they say so on the news if your culture so strongly believes in them?"

He took a deep breath before explaining, "It's likely that it is the work of the undead. Vampires have always known how to cover their tracks, so that would explain the broken necks. They will do whatever they can to walk unknown among the living. They need to blend in, especially when they sense danger, and I'm sure they can."

"Danger? What danger?"

Val answered before his father could. "Us, the vampire hunters."

"Oh, of course. Well, if there is a vampire after me, then it would sense Val's presence, and I'd be safe, right? I mean, I leave on Wednesday, and I suppose I could leave early. I might even be able to catch a flight out today."

"No!" both men yelped. "You can't leave until this is resolved. If you leave and take the Jewel of Isis with you, then we will all be at the vampire's mercy. Where there is one vampire, there will be more. It only takes one to build an army and wipe out the human race," Alim explained.

"Yeah and also, we can't protect you if it follows you home," Val added.

The room began to spin again. "But you said they don't go to America, so how can it follow me?"

Val opened his mouth to answer, but then he closed it and waited for his father to respond instead.

"This vampire has survived the wrath of Isis, making it stronger than the average vampire. We don't know what all powers it has, and we don't know what the creature might be capable of."

"Oh," she mumbled with a heavy heart. "Why hasn't the vampire attacked me then? I mean, I've been alone, so why hasn't it tried to kill me? How can you even be sure it knows I have the necklace? And for that matter, why now? The necklace has been in the museum all along, so why now while I'm here?"

Alim scowled and took a deep breath. "I can only assume that the disturbance to the necklace, when it changed hands, is what set things into motion; however, it may run deeper than that. It may specifically be because of you. You were intended to have the necklace; you were destined to be its keeper. You appear to be the guardian mentioned in the prophecy."

She wrung her hands in her lap. "Well, if there is a prophecy, and it's coming true, then how does it end? Isn't that part written too?"

He shook his head. "No, only the journey was written, not the destination." He cocked his head and stared deeply into her bulging eyes. "Have you noticed anything odd? Has someone been watching you at night?"

She gulped hard and confessed about the man outside her window, and Alim's expression tightened.

"It's likely the vampire," he sighed.

"Okay, let's go with that theory. Then let me ask again, why hasn't he attacked me?"

Alim looked at his folded hands and squeezed his eyes shut. "He might have in his own way. The vampire can seduce its victims if it wants to turn them as opposed to kill them."

"Well, no one has tried to seduce me." *Except for maybe your son.* She glanced at Val out of the corner of her eye.

"If the creature put you under its mind control, you wouldn't know it. I've read in my family's diaries that it could seem like a dream to you."

A seductive dream like the ones I've been having? A chill ran down her spine.

"What's wrong, dear?" his mother asked. "You're so pale."

"Um…I…um…I just don't feel well," she lied. "This is a lot of information to absorb."

Val's parents nodded in understanding. "You'll need to know what to do now," Alim proclaimed.

"Yes, what do I do? I obviously can't fight someone in my dreams"—she gestured to herself —"Not that I can fight a vampire while awake either."

Val snickered, but his dad kept a serious tone. "You don't have to fight the vampire; we'll do that part. As for in your dreams, I can only suggest you force yourself to maintain control."

She crossed her arms in frustration. "And how do I do that?"

"By learning the power of channeling."

She scrunched her brows together and leaned forward. "The what?"

He smiled his crooked grin at her, and it made her wonder if he was only teasing. "You must learn how to channel his powers and use them against him. Absorb his energy and reflect it back."

Hannah nibbled on her lip. "Yeah, I don't know how to do that. I don't even understand what you're saying."

He got out of his chair and crossed the room to the bookcase again. He pulled a book from the middle shelf, blew the dust off it, and handed it to her. "This book should help you. Some of my family members were able to channel, and they explain how to do it in here. I suggest you learn it as quickly as possible."

No pressure there. "Well, then I guess I should get back to my hotel, so I can read as much as possible before dark." She glanced at Val. "Can we go?"

He looked at his father and answered, "Yes, but let me grab a couple of things first. I'm not leaving you alone tonight."

"Excuse me? You're doing what?" She blinked at him with a hard stare.

He was already walking down the adjoining hallway, though. "I'm packing to stay overnight," he called out over his shoulder.

Panic widened her eyes, and her breathing became ragged. It felt like her heart was going to hammer its way out of her chest. *I can't be alone with him after my fantasizing.*

"We feel it's in your best interest if Val stays close to you—even after you have mastered channeling. It's for your safety of course," Alim explained.

*Not when there's sexual tension there...*Hannah tried to calm her breathing by mentally counting to ten. She folded and unfolded her hands in her lap while her mind raced to find a way out of the whole situation.

"Is he even trained to do anything?" she asked while rising from the couch and pacing the room again. "I know he said he's been practicing fighting, but is he ready?"

"Yes, like he said, he's been working hard on his training the last few days. Also, I believe the creature will stay away as long as it feels Val's presence. Or that is at least what I hope."

She bit her lower lip while an idea formed. "Well, maybe he can rent the room next to mine then. I don't believe it's in use."

"I'm afraid I have to be right by your side," Val exclaimed as he sauntered back into the room with a backpack.

She didn't like the grin he was wearing. With a groan, she looked down at her feet and willed them to move. He was already walking to the front door. She looked back at his father to tell him one more thing, though.

"As I said, I leave in three days, so how can we get this, whatever it is, done in time?"

Alim stood and approached her. "My guess is that you'll have to stay longer. You can't risk the vampire following you to the U.S. for the reasons mentioned earlier."

Hannah's stomach flipped and roiled. She wished she'd never volunteered to come after the necklace. She wished the world was still as she used to know it. She didn't like this new one with monsters.

Armand had shifted into a hawk to keep up with the man's car as he drove Hannah to a small house. He'd learned about cars, and many other modern-day wonders, while flying around the city during the day and listening in on conversations. He was doing what he could to learn how to fit in with the new world. He had no intentions of not surviving what was to come.

He'd perched outside the window to eavesdrop, but talismans hung all around the house to ward evil magic off, so he was unable to hear. He'd picked up tension from her body language, though, especially when the Egyptian spoke to her.

The man she addressed as Val was already going to be a formidable foe to deal with, but now he had the Egyptian to deal with too. Even though he couldn't hear them, he knew the man was Val's father because of the physical likeness, and he sensed the strength lying in their bloodline. He knew he needed to recruit others to help him.

When Hannah and Val left, he followed them back to her hotel and landed on her balcony. He chose to remain in the hawk form just in case he needed a quick escape. He kept out of sight and waited for them to get back up to her room. While he waited, he formed a plan. That night, while hunting his prey, he would hunt for a minion too.

A door slammed shut, quickly drawing his attention to the room's occupants.

"I still don't think this is necessary," Hannah moaned. "I'll be fine; otherwise, he would've already done something."

Val shook his head at her in a quiet scolding. He set his bag by her bed, causing her to throw daggers with her eyes, so he quickly picked it up and carried it to the large chair in the room.

"Yes, if you must stay, that's where you'll be spending the night," she said in a huff.

"My father explained why I'm staying with you. Why must you argue with reason?"

She felt her anger boiling over, and he was the only one around to release it on. She chucked a pillow at him while yelling, "Because none of this is reasonable! It's pure lunacy; that's what it is!"

He caught the pillow in the face, but when he responded, he was still calm. "I understand that this is difficult for you. You weren't brought up with it like I was. You are either in the wrong place at the wrong time, or you are destined for this. Either way, you're in it up to your eyeballs now, so you need to come to grips with that." He could sense her forming a retort, so he held a finger up to silence her. "The best place for you to start is with the book my father gave you. You need to learn how to channel, and I don't know how, so it's up to that book to teach you."

She ran her hand over the book's shabby cover and opened it to the middle. The pages had yellowed, and there were permanent creases where some had been marked in the corner. The dust flying off while she turned the pages made her cough and sneeze.

"God bless you," Val told her.

Her eyes were watering, so she reached for a tissue, while mumbling her thanks, and dabbed at them. She could tell different people had written in the book because some of the print was small and tight while other sections were large and loopy. Some was written in English, but most of it was written in Arabic.

"I can't read Arabic," she professed.

He smiled and reached for the book. "I can. My father taught me, so I'd be closer to his people."

Hannah narrowed her eyes at him. "So, when he gave me the book, he already knew you'd have to be here to translate. That's deceitful."

H shrugged and opened the book. "Either way, you need me. Admit it."

She clucked her tongue and sat on the bed. "I don't know about that. I could always use Google to learn more about channeling."

"Pfft. You'd learn only what people think it means. You wouldn't know the truths of it like my ancestors do."

She threw her hands up with a sigh while he pulled a chair closer to the bed. "Whatever. Tell me what it says," she relented.

She watched his mouth work without sound as he read the words to himself first. His eyebrows furrowed, making her think there were a couple he didn't know or couldn't remember.

He finally looked up with a smile. "Okay, I've got some information." He paused for dramatic effect. "Before you can learn to channel the energy of another, you must learn to channel it for yourself from the universe."

"Sounds deep," she interrupted, which earned her a glare.

"Anyway, close your eyes and hold your hands out in front of you, separated by a few inches. Turn your palms in so they face each other. Imagine an energy ball the size of a softball resting between them. You can feel its shape, size, and hardness. Now, as you imagine a beach ball, spread your hands out. Imagine how that feels. Picture other balls in varied sizes and hardness and expand or contract your hands as you do, feeling how they provide different energy waves. Feel that energy traveling up your arms, through your shoulders and neck, and into your brain each time." He quieted and let her do the exercise for several minutes. "Okay, you can open your eyes now."

She took a deep breath and let it out on a sigh. "Is that it? Are we done?"

Val smirked and shook his head. "Baby, we're just getting started."

She made a sour face. "That's unfortunate because I'm hungry. The last thing I pictured was a meatball on a huge pile of spaghetti." Her stomach growled for emphasis.

He closed the book and rose from his chair. "Okay, okay. Let's go eat because I'm hungry too. Where would you like to go? Do you want to try Alle Corone again?"

She wrinkled her nose. "I'm kind of hungry for something American, like a burger and fries."

He laughed. "Oh, the food of your people then. Okay."

"Well, maybe the burger, but the fries are French," she said and jabbed his shoulder. She didn't mean for the gesture to lead to anything, but he wrapped an arm around her waist and pulled her in.

"I want a little dessert first," he rumbled and pressed his lips to hers.

Hannah let herself get swallowed up in the heated kiss until she felt his burgeoning erection pressed against her pelvis. Then she pulled back from him.

"Okay...well...that was nice, but let's go eat," she spouted. "My treat this time."

She quickly led the way downstairs to the hotel's restaurant, which served a little bit of everything. She ordered a cheeseburger and fries, while he ordered eggplant parmesan.

"I want to the see the necklace," he blurted while she was taking a drink of her water, and she almost spit it out.

She cleaned her chin up with her cloth napkin and replied, "Oh...well...it's locked up. Besides, haven't you seen it before at the museum?"

He scowled at her. "Yes, but not since I was quite young." He took a bite of his salad before mentioning, "Anyway, you're going to need it near you. It's the only way to"—he looked around to make sure no one was listening in—"send the bloodsucker to hell where it belongs."

She narrowed her blue eyes and studied him. "Why are you looking around? I thought your culture believed, so who cares if someone heard you?"

He leaned in and whispered, "You never know who you can trust. I'll explain later."

Hannah shook her head at him. He was acting stranger than usual. Then again, her entire trip was full of strange. She looked up as the server set their plates down and refilled their water glasses. Before the man walked away, he winked at her.

"What's that smile about?" Val asked, and she felt herself blushing.

"Nothing. He smiled, so I was just smiling back."

Val stretched his neck to look at the server who was checking on another table. "The nerve," he mumbled.

"What are you talking about?"

"The nerve of him to flirt with you while you're sitting here with me." He gave her a lopsided grin and dug into his meal.

She glanced over her shoulder and then smirked back at him. "Don't all of you guys think you're Italian stallions?"

He leaned his head to the side and slowly nodded. "Yes, but in my case, it's true. Perhaps you'll let me prove it." He winked and took another bite of the eggplant.

She glowered in response, but the idea wasn't repulsive. She'd certainly been having nice dreams about him. *Or was it a dream? Alim said vampires use hypnosis to seduce…*She shook her head to clear her thoughts. Even if she was starting to believe they exist, she had no reason to believe she'd been seduced by a vampire. That would just be too much to handle, as if she didn't have enough to deal with already.

She needed to change the topic, so she asked him about his job. It turned out, he worked as a security guard for the Tropicarium Park in Jesolo.

"So, as you can see, I'm used to protecting precious things," he murmured with another wink.

"Smooth," she retorted between the last bites of her burger.

When they were finished, she wanted to go for a stroll in the early evening hours—considering she couldn't go when it was dark out, curfew or no curfew. However, he insisted they get back to studying the art of channeling.

"You need to take this seriously, and I'll even let you practice on me," he offered.

"Well, I suppose that does sweeten the pot," she sniped sarcastically.

"We'll also need the necklace, so is it in your room? I think you should put it on for your protection."

She was the one to look around for eavesdroppers this time. "How would it protect me?" she asked when they were alone in the elevator, and the doors were closed.

"I'm not sure how it works, but it is infused with Isis's magic, so I trust that it will work."

"That's all you know about it? You don't know what to expect?"

He reached out and took her hand, entwining his fingers with hers. "Think about God and Jesus. You believe in His divine power even though you can't see it, right? Well, this is the same. You need to have faith."

The doors opened, but she pushed the first-floor button to go back downstairs. When he cocked his head, she mumbled, "It's in the hotel's safe."

"Good. You're making a wise decision," he said with a smile she disliked.

For the first time, she had to wonder if he was really a jewel thief. If he was, she was putting the biggest heist right into his lap.

Sixteen

Hannah and Val entered her room with the extraordinary necklace tucked inside her purse. She immediately crossed the room to the safe where she slipped it inside with her souvenirs.

"Like I said before, you should be wearing it. It isn't going to do you any good in there," he noted.

"The sun is still up," she pointed out, "so I don't need to be wearing it now."

He crossed his arms over his chest. "I know that, but you need to form a bond with the jewel. You need to learn how to use its power."

She shook her head and sighed out of frustration. "Look, I need to do one thing at a time. Your father said to learn channeling, so I'm starting with that." She sat back on the bed and opened the book to where they'd left off. She laid it opened in front of him and tapped the page. "What does this say?"

He looked at her from under hooded eyes and picked the book up. "You need to be one with the earth. You need to harness the energy from its core. Close your eyes and imagine being bound to it and the universe with an invisible rope. It runs the length of your body and extends to the sky. It holds you in place. It gives you the power you seek.

"Now connect it to the ball of energy you held earlier. Feel them entwining around you and filling your body with strength, with power, and with clarity. You can feel them connecting to your aura, wrapping you in strength. Feel its heat, its heaviness, and its elasticity.

"Hold your palms out in front of you. Feel the heat moving through them. When you can feel it, stretch your arms out farther, and feel the heat traveling with them to stretch around you. It's strong. It's protective. It's a shield for you. Your power lies within your aura."

While he watched, Hannah moved her arms in and out. He could tell she was concentrating hard because of the facial expressions she made.

"Open your eyes, Hannah," he whispered.

She blinked rapidly and looked around the room. "That was weird. I could feel what you described."

He smiled and patted her leg. "Excellent. That means you're learning to channel the energy around you."

"Okay, well, then what? What do I do with it?"

He glanced down at the book and flipped the page, reading silently to himself for a couple of minutes. "It's only the first step," he stated and kept reading.

"It's the first step to what?" She fluffed her pillows and leaned her back against them.

He closed the book and looked at her. "It's the first step in learning to channel, so you'll be able to channel the power of the vampire. But first, you'll need to practice with me. We'll start practicing on you channeling my energy tomorrow."

She looked out the window at the blackened sky. "Why not do it now?"

He put the book on top of the television and stretched. "Because I don't want to overwhelm you with too much too soon. You should learn it in pieces and have time to practice it before you'll need it." He approached her side of the bed. "Besides, I'm too tired to keep going tonight."

She agreed with a yawn. "Me too."

She climbed out of bed and went into the bathroom to brush her teeth and wash her face. She considered taking a shower, but that would be weird with him in the other room. The necklace was securely locked up in the safe, but she didn't know if she trusted the lock on the bathroom door. Of course, he was in her room for the whole night, and she'd be vulnerable while sleeping too, so she reconsidered.

"Do you need to use the bathroom before I take a shower?" she asked.

"Yes, please." He grabbed his toothbrush and took care of his business. When he returned, he told her, "I'm going to try to go to sleep, but I'll be alert if the creature shows his fangs around here."

She studied him carefully. "And what will you do? Did you pack holy water, crucifixes, garlic, or a wooden stake?"

He laughed. "I just might have. Try not to worry so much; it will cause wrinkles."

"Mmm-hmm. Good night," she mumbled and went back inside the bathroom.

After her shower, she dressed in a clean T-shirt and pair of shorts. When she stepped back into the main room, she found Val sound asleep in the chair, which he'd moved across the room, so it was close to both the balcony and the entrance. His shirt was off, and she saw that he was wearing a talisman that was in the shape of an eye with a bird on one side and a snake on the other. It didn't look like the cat's eye Maria wore; it looked more Egyptian.

She climbed into bed, leaving the lamp on. She couldn't fall asleep in the low lighting, though, so she turned it off ten minutes later. It still took several minutes to drift off, but once she finally did, she was whisked off to the dream realm.

Seventeen

Armand was perched on the vixen's balcony rail. Her protector was wearing a talisman that kept him at a safe distance, at least while shifted. He didn't think it would be strong enough to keep him at bay while in vampire form.

He waited until they were both asleep to shift back. He stared at her sleeping form with lust mounting in his loins. If only she didn't have her guard dog there, they could both enjoy the pleasures of the night. He almost turned to leave when an idea occurred to him.

He focused his mind on her and stepped inside her dreams.

She was wandering through the city streets of Venice, nervously scanning the shadows for untold horrors. He watched her at first, admiring the swish and sway of the long blue dress she wore. Blue wasn't his preference, though, so he changed the dress to a shorter, lace lined, scarlet one that dipped low toward her breasts.

She noticed the change and became flustered. He could hear her heart racing, and it sang to him. He licked his fangs at the thought of her sweet, warm blood coursing through her healthy veins and pouring down his dry throat.

He stepped out of the shadows, catching her eye, and crooked his finger to her. "Come to me, my beauty. Come here, and let me taste your lips."

Hannah stepped forward, not of her own will, but of his. She couldn't stop her feet from moving her toward the dark shadowy figure. His voice was velvety and sexy, drawing her in. At first, she thought it was Val, but as she got closer, she saw that it wasn't. This man was bigger than

Val, and his voice was seductive. She stopped just before him and looked up. She knew she should run, but her feet were plastered to the ground with invisible bindings. Her arms involuntarily rose to place her palms on his steely chest.

"Who are you?" she whispered in a softer voice than what she intended.

"Tonight, I'm your lover, my beauty. On another night, I'll be your savior."

He leaned down and pressed his cool lips to hers, moving them enough to make her mouth open for his tongue. She didn't want to let him kiss her, but she was under his spell. He made her want things she shouldn't, and his tongue played with hers, exploring the shadows of her mouth. He realized she must've grazed his fangs while kissing him back because a gasp caught in her throat.

He moved his mouth away and trailed it down her neck. His thirst demanded he bury his fangs into the sweet carotid pulsing beneath his kisses, but the throbbing in his loins demanded he bury his flesh too. That won out.

He suckled on her neck, without piercing it, while unzipping her dress. He let it fall to her waist, baring her breasts.

"No, we shouldn't do this," she protested.

He didn't stop his caressing of her nipples, though. "You don't really want me to stop, do you?" he purred seductively.

"No, I don't," she relented.

He chuckled softly. "I didn't think so." He pushed her dress the rest of the way down, followed by her panties. "That's better," he murmured and ran his fingertips over her mound. "You're so soft, my beauty."

Her hand had strayed to his groin, where she clasped it around him. "You're so hard," she moaned. "Oh, Val."

"No!" he hissed and forced her chin up so she had to look at him. "Armand, not Val. Say it!"

She cocked her head in confusion and stared at him through hazy eyes. "Armand? Who are you? Why are you here?" she asked with tremors in her voice.

He stroked his long fingers over her cheek with one hand while his other held her arm to keep her from bolting. "As I said before, I'm your lover tonight."

"Oh, I see," she whispered, entranced by his stare.

He unbuttoned his trousers and let his throbbing rod spring free. She looked down and clasped him with one hand. He groaned when she began to stroke him. It was time.

He wrapped his arm around her and leaned her back until she was on the ground. Lying on top of her, he took her right bud into his mouth and nipped with his regular teeth. Holding off on her blood would make it all the sweeter when he drank it. She screamed with need and bucked her hips beneath him.

He put himself at her damp opening and pushed until he was most of the way inside. Leaning back from her, he took one of her legs and placed it on his shoulder to allow his shaft more of her body. He was in so deep now, enjoying the velvety feel of her. As he flexed his hips, he nipped her ankle with his fangs and suckled the warm, sweet blood trickling out. She cried out when he bit her, but she didn't act frightened, and she didn't pull her leg away. He grabbed her other leg and put it over his arm. Then he leaned forward, pushing her knees toward her chest. He felt her climax all around him, and it pulled him to his own culmination. Owning her body again like that was helping him with his main goal.

He let her get dressed, before he told her what he wanted. "Let's go back to your hotel room, and I'll give you more," he moaned against her ear.

"More? Really?" Her voice was husky, laced with lust.

"Mmm, a lot more," he promised.

"Okay," she softly cried.

He wrapped his arms around her and concentrated on her hotel room. They were suddenly standing in the middle of the room, and Val was still asleep in the chair, while her body was on the bed. He was glad to see that he was right about the talisman—it wasn't strong enough to keep him away.

Armand leaned over her sleeping form and whispered in her ear, "Aprite lentamente gli occhi, ma restate nella tua trance." *Slowly open your eyes, but stay in your trance.*

Her eyes fluttered open, and the dream version of her was gone like a vapor.

"Climb out of bed," Armand told her, and she obeyed without question. "Now take this and go to him." He handed her an athamé. She hesitated before taking the dagger, though. "Take it. It's all right. I'm here to help you."

She fingered the handle and then clasped her hand around it. "Why do I need this?" she whispered while turning it over to examine it.

"He's here to harm you. He plans on killing you," he replied with a straight face; although, he was smiling on the inside. Killing the man himself would be a treat, but having her do it for him would help with her conversion.

"I don't know. He seems harmless enough," she whispered.

"He wants your necklace. He wants to steal it from you, and he'll kill you to do it. Trust me," he assured her.

"The necklace," she gasped. "He's a thief."

"Yes, my beauty, he's a thief. Now take care of him," he instructed.

She leaned over Val with the dagger held up high, ready to plunge it into his chest. Her presence made him stir, though, and his eyes flew open.

"What are you doing, Hannah?" he asked with a yawn.

She looked at her hand, which was raised up over his body, and it was empty. She looked to where Armand was standing, but he was gone. It had just been a dream, and she sighed with relief.

"I...I...I don't know," she said. "I think I was sleepwalking." She looked down at her clothes and saw that the dress was gone; she was wearing a T-shirt and shorts. "I was dreaming, and then I...don't know." She didn't fully understand what had happened, and she'd never walked in her sleep before either.

"Oh, well, it's the middle of the night, so you should go back to sleep. We both need our rest. Unless..." He rose from the chair and stepped toward her, slinking an arm around her waist. "Unless you want to do something else."

He leaned in, and his mouth worked over hers, engulfing her in a probing kiss. His tongue slipped between her lips, which were parted in surprise, and made sweeping, swirling motions inside her mouth. She hesitated at first, but then gave in and let him continue his onslaught. After the erotic part of her dream, which she clearly recalled, she needed it. Getting naked with him was just a formality now.

She ran her hand over his chest while his moved up under her T-shirt to cup her left breast. She hadn't put her bra back on after her shower, so he took her nipple between his fingers and squeezed. She moaned into his mouth, encouraging him to do more.

He broke the kiss off and pulled her shirt up and over her head. His mouth moved to where his hand had been playing, and he sucked her nipple in. She grabbed a handful of his hair, pulling him into her, and gasped with pleasure as he suckled harder.

Val pushed her pants and underwear down with one swoop, and she stepped out of them. He scooped her naked body up and carried her to the bed. She heard the zipper of his fly as he shrugged out of his pants, and her excitement mounted until the only thing she heard was the blood pounding in her ears. He climbed into the bed without a word and nuzzled his head between her thighs.

Hannah moaned as he pushed her legs apart, and moved his mouth intimately over her petal-softness. She felt herself go up in flames as he brought her to rapture.

"Oh God, that feels good. Fuck me," she begged. Her hips were already bucking off the bed, demanding that he fill her body.

"All right," he grunted and rose above her. He prodded her passage a few times to make sure she was ready, and then he plunged in. "Is this what you want?"

"Yes," she replied with a pant. "Give it to me good."

She moved her body in rhythm with his, but it was bitter disappointment. He was much better in her dreams. It still felt nice, but the wow factor was gone. He quickly climaxed with a loud moan and rolled off her. She couldn't help but be glad he was at least good with his mouth.

She cleaned herself up and re-dressed in the bathroom before she climbed back into bed, where he still lay naked. He rolled over and wrapped his arm around her with his groin pressed firmly against her buttocks.

Instead of falling back to sleep, she stared at the shadows in the corner, trying to piece back together the bizarre dream. *It had seemed all too real.*

Eighteen

Armand was scouring the city for food and a minion to do his bidding. He had no one particular in mind for his meal, but when he saw a busty woman with hair as dark as the night sky, he knew she was the one. She would be his dinner.

He swooped in on her like an eclipse, blacking out the nearby streetlight with a simple wave of his hand. There would be no one to see her unfortunate demise. No one would hear her scream.

He was going to make it a quick attack, but then he caught the scent of her pheromones, and his staff grew hard yet again. Nothing would stop him from taking her body while he took her life's blood.

He pulled her in tightly against his steel-like frame. "You seem to be lost, my pretty," he murmured while running his finger down her cheek.

"Hi, handsome. Are you looking for a date?" she purred without fear.

He laughed low in his throat. "You could say that." His finger made a path down her neck, and he used his nail to nick her flesh enough to spill blood, which he quickly tasted.

"Hey," she scolded, "I'm not into that freaky shit. If you want something unusual, it's going to cost you extra. But since you're so handsome, I'll give you a discount." She wet her lips and batted her heavy lashes in the dark, but he saw the seductive move with his vampire eyes.

He squeezed her arm until the bone almost snapped. "I'll take everything I want."

She tried to yank her arm away, but his grip was like a vice. "You don't have to be rough, fella. We'll still have a good time." She ran her experienced hand over his hard bulge and clucked her tongue. "Mmm…a very good time."

He forced her up against the brick building behind her, pushed her skirt up, yanked her panties down, and forced himself inside her. She felt nothing like Hannah, and it made him cringe with disgust, but he didn't stop. He sank his teeth into her shoulder, tasting grime and tobacco smoke residue, while he pumped her with hard strokes. She cried out when he pierced her flesh, but she maintained a firm clutch on him, urging him to keep pounding her. He drained her of blood while he filled her with his seed, and then he discarded her with a snapped neck, just like the others.

Now that his hunger and lust were slaked, it was time to find his minion. It didn't take long to cross paths with a vendor who was packing up his wares for the night. He approached the dumpy man with purpose in his stride.

"Sorry, pal," the man tossed over his shoulder, "I'm done for the day because of the damn curfew. The fucking cops are ruining business for all of us." He pulled the doors closed on his cart and put the padlock on, throwing a quick glance at Armand who stood still and quiet. "You should get going too, pal."

Armand broke his silence with a low throaty laugh. "I know nothing of a curfew, and I could care less about cops."

"Where the hell have you been not to know about the curfew? Are you from out of town or something?"

Armand laughed again and stepped closer to the man. "More like out of time." He put his hand around the man's throat and lifted him off the ground.

The portly man struggled, flailing his arms and kicking his legs, but he couldn't shake the grip on his thick neck. It was much like the clutch of a boa constrictor. He tried to yell for help, but his voice came out as a gurgle.

Since his point was made, Armand set the man back on his feet, but he shoved him against the cart and held him firmly in place.

"What are y-you going to do to me?" he squawked.

Armand smiled, knowing the man could see his fangs from the glow of the streetlamp. "I'm going to give you the job of a lifetime."

He sank his fangs into the man's thick neck and pulled on the salty blood. He didn't take much; he only took what he needed to assert his control, which was a good thing because the pungent fluid offended his palate.

He leaned away from the man and stared into his glassy eyes. "Don't you feel better now?"

"Yes, master." The man stared blankly into Armand's hypnotic eyes.

"What is your name?" Armand asked.

"I'm Tony, master."

Armand let go of the man and stepped backward. "Come, Tony. Let's get started. You have much to learn about your new role in life."

He decided he would have his lackey fetch him another woman first. He needed to get the man's taste out of his mouth.

Nineteen

Hannah awoke Monday morning to the sound of the television, and it made her jump as she realized she wasn't alone. Then the previous day flooded back to her, and she focused her eyes on Val, who was sitting in a chair at the small table. They'd had sex, and that changed everything.

"Good morning," he greeted her. "Sorry if I woke you with the television."

"Um, no, it's okay. I never sleep in late." *Except for the last couple of days.* "Will you turn the news on?"

He grabbed the remote and flipped channels until a local broadcast came on. The reporter grimly announced that two more female victims had been discovered with broken necks in Venice. He brought up the 9:00 curfew, expressing how important it was to adhere to it, and he reiterated that the police had no suspects yet.

"Shit! We've got to do something," Val hissed and turned off the TV. "Let's practice channeling some more. The sooner you learn it, the sooner this can all be just a bad memory. Then if he doesn't come here and attack, we'll find his lair and attack him."

She wished she had his optimism because she couldn't help but feel like she was heading to her own funeral. She carried clean clothes into the bathroom and took care of her morning routine. When she reemerged, she announced that she wanted to order breakfast before they did any more practicing.

"Okay, but let's at least practice until it arrives," he suggested.

"I need a gallon of coffee first. I'm exhausted," she mumbled and approached the coffee maker.

He smirked at her. "It must be from all the sleepwalking you did last night. Do you do that often?"

She twisted a strand of hair around her finger. "No, I've not done it since I was a little girl. Even then, I only did it two or three times."

His face twisted in thought. "Well, can you remember what you were dreaming about."

She pretended to think about it. She remembered, but she couldn't very well tell him that she'd dreamed she was going to kill him because a stranger told her to. So, instead, she opted for, "I don't remember much. I can only recall walking around outside."

She reached down to scratch her ankle, which had been itching since she got up. She examined the area and saw two small red blotches, and part of the dream flooded back to her. Her dream lover had bitten her there. *Coincidence?* She couldn't shake what Alim Aleron had said. He'd told her a vampire could seduce her through hypnosis. He'd said, "it could seem like a dream to you." She shivered and earned a questioning glance from Val.

"What's that about? It's hardly cold in here."

She opened her mouth to answer, although she didn't know what to say, when a knock on the door saved her. Room service was there with breakfast.

While they ate in silence, she ran through the dream in her mind to figure out if it could've been a hypnotic trance. As much as she didn't want to admit the dream to Val, she knew she had to. She needed his advice.

"Um…I think I remember my dream now," she began. "But after what your father said, I have to wonder if it was a dream at all. I'm so confused right now."

His eyes bulged, and he stopped eating. "Go on. Tell me what happened."

"Well, I was outside, walking around town, when someone stepped out of the shadows. I thought it was you at first, but it wasn't. I think he said his name was Armand.

Anyway, he…he…seduced me." Her voice had lowered, and Val had to strain to hear her.

"Okay, what else?"

She felt her face go up in flames, and a tightness grew in her chest. The second part was even harder to admit. "He told me you were going to kill me to get the necklace, but he would help me. Then he gave me a dagger and told me to kill you."

His eyes went wide again, and the olive tone drained from his face. He pulled his phone out of his pocket and pressed a series of keys.

"Dad, something has happened. We need your advice," he insisted.

Hannah paced the room while Val explained her dream to Alim. She felt claustrophobic, so she stepped out onto her balcony, closing the door behind her. She took several deep breaths of the mid-morning air to try to relax, but it did little good. She wanted to wake up from the nightmare and be home again. She longed for the mundane life she'd thought she needed a vacation from. Nothing would ever be the same now, and that's if she survived the madness.

The door slid open, and Val stepped out. Without saying anything, he pulled her into a hug.

"Is it that bad?" she cried against his shoulder.

She felt emotion radiating from him before he confirmed her suspicion. "It's not good."

She pulled out of his embrace and sat down in one of the two chairs. "Be straight with me; I can handle it."

He sat in the other chair and clasped his hands. He looked at them instead of her. "The vampire had the opportunity to take your life, but he didn't."

"Okay, so you agree it wasn't a dream. Why did he spare my life then? What does he have to gain?" She already formed an assumption, but she needed to hear him say it.

"A mate." He slapped his palm on the table. "Either he's playing with us, or he's trying to turn you. Of course, the latter theory is the most likely scenario"—he looked up at her—"Also, it seems he can control your dreams by projecting into them. It's a form of mind control, and only the strongest vampires have the ability."

She chewed her bottom lip, trying not to burst into tears. "We already knew he was strong. He survived the wrath of Isis, right?"

He bobbed his head, and his face was grim. "Yes, we did, but we didn't know he was *that* strong."

Hannah rose from the chair and paced the deck. "So, what are you saying exactly? Are you saying there's nothing that can be done? Are we all screwed?"

His hesitation made her even more terrified. "My father doesn't think so. He thinks if we ban together, we can stop the creature. However, we have to act before he can finish converting you, and you can help with that."

Her voice was shrill, and some nearby pigeons scattered. "How? How the hell can I help stop him? And what if I can't? What will happen to me then?"

He jerked his head back at the piercing sound. "By learning to channel his powers, Hannah. You're doing well with learning it so far, and I'm sure you'll have it down in no time flat. As for what happens if we fail, let's not discuss that. I intend to win this battle." He got up and strode across the balcony to embrace her again. "It will be all right. I won't let him hurt you."

Hannah yanked herself free from his hold. "Val, we need to talk about what happened last night."

He stared into her eyes, trying to read what she was feeling, and his mouth turned down in a deep scowl. "You're going to say it didn't mean anything, aren't you?"

She broke their eye contact and looked down at her trembling hands. "Well, kind of, yeah. I mean, it meant *something* but not what I think you're hoping for."

He sighed and stepped away from her. The movement was small, but the change in the atmosphere was huge. She could tell that he was the kind of person who wore his heart on his sleeve, and she felt guilty.

"It's okay. After all, you warned me," he mumbled and went back inside the room.

She started to follow him but stopped in her tracks. Pressing the issue would just cause him further embarrassment. She continued to pace the balcony, looking toward the canal. She looked at the vendors with their carts full of wares that they were pushing to tourists, and she noticed one of the vendors looking back in her direction. She didn't put much thought into it, though, since vampires can't roam in the daylight.

She turned toward the door to go back inside to work on channeling. She had to be proactive if she expected to keep herself from joining the undead.

Twenty

Armand circled the sky while Hannah and Val sat on her balcony. He caught the exchange between them, when the man had tried to embrace her, and it ruffled his feathers. He noticed that she didn't return the affectionate hug, however, and that gave him smug satisfaction. She obviously preferred his touch over the other man's.

He flew toward Tony and landed by his cart after Hannah went back inside her room. He wanted to eavesdrop, but the man was wearing his talisman, and it deflected his powers. It gave him an idea, though. He'd just have his minion steal it. He used his powers of telepathy to implant the thought in Tony's subconscious mind. Normally, when shifted, he didn't have the power to do that; however, with a minion, there was a strong mental link present, so it was easy enough to do.

"Yes, master. I'll get the necklace and destroy it," Tony mumbled to the bird. He kept his voice low so passersby didn't overhear him talking to a crow. "I'll watch for him to leave the hotel, and I'll get it."

Armand flew back to her balcony. He might not be able to overhear their conversation, but he could still read her body language, and what a beautiful body it was. He shuddered from just thinking about her warm flesh. He needed to have her again, which meant he needed to get her friend out of her hotel room. The full moon was coming that night, too.

Twenty-one

Hannah sat on the bed and told Val, "I'm ready to study some more. Lay it on me."

He looked up from the dusty book with a crooked smile. "I'm glad you're taking this seriously. It's important that you learn to call on the power of the necklace, so you can destroy the vampire."

She held up her hand to stop him. "Just a minute. Hold the phone. I have to destroy the vampire? What the hell happened to you being an all-powerful warrior who would teach him a lesson? Since when did this fall into my lap?" Her voice would shatter glass if it was one octave higher.

He closed the book and leveled his gaze on her. "It's a combination of the two of us. I can fight him, but *you* are the only one who can use the necklace to destroy him. I can't access its power, only you can. It chose you as the new guardian."

Shit. For once, I'd like to be picked last.

He opened the book up to the last page they'd worked on. "Let's go back over what you've already learned and start there. Close your eyes and concentrate on your breathing. See the energy ball in your mind's eye and clasp it. Then picture the rope holding you to the ground and sending energy through you. Feel your aura surrounding you and strengthen it. Protect yourself from outside forces with it. It's your shield to use as you need, and you can feel it growing." He watched her reaching out to feel it surrounding her. "Now, we're going to open your third eye. It lies between your eyebrows above your eyes. It's closed now, but you can use your energy to open it. Feel it slowly opening. Imagine what you can see with it. You don't just see your surroundings, you see the energy floating around you. You can see other people's auras. Try seeing mine."

He watched her brows knit together, and she sucked her bottom lip in.

"I'm going to reach for you, but you're going to use your aura and your third eye to push me away. Feel your strength and resist me, but keep your other eyes closed. Just use the center one. Use your chakra."

He slowly reached a hand toward her, and she slapped it away. He reached again, but from a different angle, and she slapped it away. He made sure her eyes were still closed before continuing.

"You're doing a good job. Make sure you keep your eyes closed. Cheating will do you no good in this exercise."

He continued to reach for her from different directions, speeding up as he did so, and she continued to slap his hand away each time.

"Excellent job! This time, don't use your hands. Instead, you will use your invisible energy shield to deflect me."

He reached for her, and his hand nudged her shoulder. "Concentrate harder," he advised and reached again. This time, he touched her neck.

Her eyes flew open, and frown lines creased her forehead. "I can't do it," she pouted and punched the mattress.

He stroked her other arm and spoke in soothing tones. "You can do it. You're doing great so far. It just takes practice."

Hannah jerked her arm away from his invading touch and clasped her hands in her lap. Subconsciously, she made a mental comparison between his touch and the vampire lover's, causing a shudder to rip through her. She met his stare and spoke her mind.

"I appreciate you staying home from work today and helping me, but I need some time alone, please. I've seen a lot of unbelievable shit since I arrived, and I need some quiet time to process it on my own terms. I'd also like to practice alone for a bit. Do you mind?"

His mouth turned down. "No, I understand. I'll need to come back before dark, though, so we can practice some more and try it with the necklace."

She glanced toward the safe, asking him, "Do you think it will have any effect on you? I thought its sole purpose was to ward off vampires."

Val shrugged. "You're probably right that it won't have an effect on me, but I still think you'll notice an increase in your power when you're wearing it. I think you'll feel the connection you're meant to have."

She laced her fingers together and stretched her arms out in front of her. "I hope so. I'll call you when I'm ready for you to come back over, okay?"

He rose from the chair and headed to the door with only a nod. She had hurt his feelings, and it made her feel like an ass.

Val walked along the sidewalk by the waterfront, oblivious to the short, plump man following him. He was perusing the multitude of carts where vendors were hawking their wares. Then he made the mistake of walking through a narrow alley with no one else around. Well, no one but Tony, who crept up behind him with a large stone.

Tony threw the stone at the man's head, hearing a loud crack when it struck. The man immediately fell to the ground, and the minion cut the talisman off his neck and disappeared back into the shadows before someone saw him. He had no idea if the man was alive or not, but he wasn't going to wait around to find out. His master would be pleased.

Twenty-two

Hannah paced the hotel room, feeling restless. When her feet grew tired, she lay on the bed and closed her eyes. She took deliberate deep breaths and focused on channeling the energy around her. She tried to see the room through her third eye, but it was hard to practice without Val's encouragement, so she worked on her aura. She imagined the field of energy being made of steel, encasing her with protection. It didn't take long for her to unintentionally fall asleep.

Armand was watching her from the balcony through a tiny sliver between the closed curtains with his beady bird eyes. He heard her soft snores when she fell asleep, and he decided to try something. He shifted into a large black wolf. With the telekinetic power of his larger brain, he opened the locked sliding door and stepped inside. He paused when she stirred from the noise, but her eyes never opened, and her snoring resumed. He closed the curtained door, once again casting the room in shadows, and shifted into his vampire body. Avoiding the crack of light coming in through the window, he approached the bed with soundless footsteps. He turned on the lamp, so she could see her lover, and he could see her pleasure reflected in her eyes.

He demanded, "Aprite gli occhi per godervi il tuo sogno. Non puoi resistere a me." *Open your eyes to enjoy your dream. You can't resist me.*

Her blue eyes fluttered open as did her mouth in surprise. "You," she whispered. "You're back."

He stroked the back of his fingers against her cheek and down her delicate neck. "I'll always come back to you. Do you want me?" He ran one finger down her bodice, pausing between her breasts.

She fought to resist him, but it was difficult. "Am I dreaming? Where's Val? He was supposed to be here."

"Yes, my beauty, you're only dreaming. You're dreaming of me," he purred.

She looked around while his hand slid under her shirt and bra to capture her rosy tip between his fingers. She noticed the sliver of light streaming across the floor and jerked her head toward the window.

"It's daytime still"—she focused her eyes on his face, which was handsome and hazed with lust—"I must be dreaming then."

The pinch on her ripened bud sent an electric current through her veins, and it went right to her core. There was no stopping her from enjoying this. It was just a dream after all. She could take her time and fully relish his company.

She pulled herself up and tugged her shirt off. He stared at her chest, and her bra's front clasp opened without him even touching it.

She looked down in surprise. "How did you do that?"

He smiled, showing off his fangs, and seductively purred, "It's part of my powers."

She finished removing the bra and then pulled her shorts and underwear off while he stripped down, baring his fully engorged flesh. He left his shirt on, though, so she tugged on it.

"Take this off too. I want to see your body. I want to feel your skin on mine," she whispered huskily.

He hesitated at first, but then he obliged. In the lamplight, she saw large scars on his muscular chest, and she reached out to trace the biggest one with her finger.

"What happened to you?"

He clasped her wrist, pulling her hand away. "Nothing you need to worry about." He pushed her backward onto the bed, pinning both of her arms over her head with one of his massive hands.

She made a soft pleasurable sound and grinned at him. "That's hot," she moaned.

He smiled back with his fangs exposed. "I want dominance over your body. Give yourself to me willingly, Hannah."

She bit her bottom lip with a smirk. "Take me. I want you to have your way with me."

He took the head of his swollen shaft and stroked her velvety folds with it. "Is this what you want, my beauty?" She answered with her hips by pressing upward toward him. "Mmm, I'll give you what you need," he growled sensuously and slid himself inside her welcoming heat.

She cried out and bucked her hips passionately underneath him. This was sex. This was what she needed. He leaned down to claim her lips in a fiery kiss, and she moaned into his sensuous mouth. She sucked on the tip of his tongue and even gave it a little nip. A low throaty growl erupted from him, and he gave her harder strokes, causing her to violently climax as his body slapped against hers.

"Let my wrists go. I want to touch you," she cried out. When he acquiesced, she dug her fingers into his rock-hard ass, pulling him into her.

Armand did his best to hold back on his hunger for her crimson nectar. He was kissing down her neck, and her pulse pounded in his ears. Her honeysuckle aroma filled his nostrils while he ran his tongue over her sweltering flesh to her breasts. He captured her left peak in between his lips and sucked hard.

In between her cries of pleasure, she gasped, "Let me turn over. I want you to take me from behind."

A cool draught blew over her wet bud, causing a shiver to run down her spine. She rolled over and pulled herself up on all fours. He didn't hesitate to bury himself back inside her velvety tunnel, but it was more exquisite in this position. He had deeper access to her, and lights exploded behind her closed eyes as he stroked to give them both indescribable pleasure.

She screamed into the pillow as waves of ecstasy crashed over her. Her orgasms were more frequent and intense this time, almost to the point of agony. She was riding yet another wave when she suddenly felt a stinging sensation in her shoulder. It startled her, and she lurched forward.

"Oh," she belted out, looking to the window for the stream of daylight streaking in. It was a beacon of reassurance that she was dreaming, so she could just let it take her wherever it wanted to go. She didn't have to fight it.

She leaned back against his mouth while he suckled her blood. "Are you turning me into…into…a vampire?" she groaned.

"Yes, I am. Then we can do this whenever we want. We can do anything we want for all eternity."

He let out a low growl while thrusting rapidly into her. She knew he was close, so she ground her buttocks against him to help him out. When he was done filling her with his milky essence, he planted kisses down her spine and rolled off to her side.

She flopped against him with her head on his chest, slowly tracing her finger over his scars. "Are you going to keep plaguing my dreams?" she asked wistfully.

He chuckled and rolled out of the bed to start re-dressing. "I'll come to you any time you desire, and this wasn't a dream." When her jaw dropped with a sharp breath, he winked at her. Then in front of her bulging eyes, he shifted back into the wolf, willed the balcony door open, and exited the room.

Hannah jumped out of the bed with the blanket wrapped around her. She watched while the wolf became a crow and flew away. She stood there for several minutes in a muddled daze. She wasn't sure if she was dreaming or not, but she had a scary and nagging suspicion that she wasn't. That left important questions. *Can all vampires appear during the day, or just him? How can I ever fight him off when he tricks me and makes my body sing?*

Twenty-three

Hannah was sitting on the bed, quietly reflecting on her afternoon with the vampire, when a knock on the door made her jump. She looked at the clock and saw that it was 4:30. Figuring it was Val, who didn't wait for her to call first, she plodded listlessly to the door. When she opened it, she had a large bouquet of flowers thrust at her by a man she didn't recognize.

"Good afternoon, mademoiselle. These are for you," the strange man announced.

She accepted the pink roses and replied, "Grazie. These are gorgeous." She gave the man a nice smile. "Let me get your tip. Just a second."

He waved her off, though. "No need to tip me, mademoiselle. That has already been taken care of." He bowed his head to her and turned to walk back down the hallway.

She searched for the card to see what Val had written. It read "Questo pomeriggio era magico," but he didn't sign it. She fetched her Italian dictionary and deciphered the message. *This afternoon was magical.* Her hand violently shook, and she dropped the card. She had so many questions and needed the right person to answer them. She needed to get together with Maria.

She waited in the café foyer for Maria to show, and she couldn't help but think she was sweating more than a hooker in church. She'd have to confess everything if she wanted answers.

"Sorry, I'm running late," Maria said as she came through the door.

Hannah shook her head. "It's all right; I just arrived too. Can we sit over there?" She pointed to a table for two in a quiet corner. Privacy was vital for their conversation.

Maria vigorously nodded with a big smile, and they made their way to the table. A barista followed them and poured their coffee.

"I'm glad you called," Maria said. "You go home soon, right?"

Hannah shrugged. "Actually, I'm not sure. Some strange things have been happening that I need to talk to you about, and it may keep me here longer."

Maria leaned in attentively. "Oh?"

Hannah took a deep breath to steady her nerves, but it didn't quite work. She still felt sweaty and flushed. "It has to do with that legend of the necklace. I have reason to believe it's true."

Maria choked on her sip of coffee and made the cross sign over her chest while rapidly speaking in Italian. "Oh, dear," she exclaimed in English. "I wondered if the stories passed down by my family would come true, but I didn't expect it to involve you."

Hannah swallowed hard, and she was sure Maria heard the gulping sound. She tried to pick up her coffee cup, but she was trembling too much, and some spilled onto the small table.

"What are the stories? What do they say exactly?" She glanced around them to make sure they still had privacy.

Maria looked too. "As I told you last week, my ancestors were Gypsies, and they had many legends. One in particular claimed that one day, a powerful creature of the night would roam the earth for the second time. It would be on a mission to destroy the Jewel of Isis and everyone who protected it. If the creature wasn't stopped, it would create others and flood the earth with its kind." She paused to take a sip of coffee.

"How can it be stopped?" Hannah whispered.

Maria clasped her cat's eye talisman. "It was written that only the guardian of the necklace would be able to stop the vampire." She paused again and took another sip of her coffee. Then she forced a smile. "I suppose that you must be the guardian."

Hannah let out a deep sigh. "So I've been told. But how do I use the necklace? Please tell me the instructions are somewhere in that legend."

Maria shrugged. "I'm sorry, but that's all I know." She thoughtfully glanced at Hannah's hands. "Although, I'd like to try something. I haven't practiced it in years, but I used to read palms, and I was fairly good at it."

Hannah stretched her right hand out, "Okay, sure. I'll take any help I can get at this point."

Maria took her hand and traced her finger over the lines in Hannah's palm. "You have three prominent lines. The longest one is you, and the other two are loves entwined around you."

"But I'm not in love with anyone," Hannah protested.

"I understand, but they may be in love with you. This point right here"—she tapped where the three lines all intersected—"is a major conflict. There will be a big struggle for your love."

Hannah pulled her hand back like it was on fire and examined her palm. She traced the three lines herself. "This could also be about something in the far future, though, right? It doesn't have to be now."

Maria shrugged. "Yes, I suppose, but there's no way to know for certain."

Hannah shook her head, causing her hair to spill over her shoulder. "It has to be. I mean, how can a vampire love?"

Again, the other woman shrugged. "Magical beings are beyond our understanding. If the vampire plans to turn you…" Hannah's wide-eyed expression made her stop short. "What is it, dear?"

She had to come completely clean with Maria if she really wanted her help and advice. So, with a deep breath, she explained about Val, about the channeling, and about her passionate encounters with her nemesis, the vampire.

Maria just stared with her mouth gaping, so Hannah felt the need to probe, "Well, what do you think?"

The Italian shook her head. "I think you're playing with fire, and you're going to get scorched."

Hannah rested her head in her hands. "So, what do I do then?" she wept. "How do I fix this and get out alive?"

"Maybe you should look to the church for help; you should discuss this with Father Patrick. I'll go with you to make it easier."

Hannah bobbed her head in agreement. Maybe the church would know how she could save the human race and her soul.

Twenty-four

Hannah slowly approached the ornate church with Maria, who was several steps ahead of her. She was terrified of what Father Patrick would have to say about her situation. Even if he believed her, would he be able to assist? She knew one thing for certain: she wasn't telling him she'd had sex with a vampire.

Maria opened the heavy door, and the squeaky hinges echoed through the empty church. She smiled at Hannah and waved for her to step inside.

"Come on, dear. There's nothing to be afraid of in here," she claimed in a soothing voice.

Actually, I'm afraid I might burst into flames. Hannah nodded and took a hesitant step inside the vestibule with her eyes closed.

"Hello, Maria," a woman greeted them.

"Hello, Sister Catherine. Is Father Patrick here this afternoon?" Maria asked for them.

The middle-aged nun shook her head. "I'm afraid not. He's visiting the orphanage today. Can I help you with something?" She eyed both women and clasped her hands in front of her.

"Actually, you might be able to help. Can we talk someplace private?" Maria inquired.

The nun nodded and motioned for them to follow her. She took them into a meeting room behind the sanctuary, and they all sat down at a large oak table.

Maria began, "Sister Catherine, we need help with a delicate situation. There is a demon among us, and he's after Hannah." She gestured to the frightened blond.

The nun's brown eyes widened, and her pale lips parted. "Please explain."

"How familiar are you with the legend of the Jewel of Isis?" Maria began.

The nun's face went blank. "I'm afraid I'm not familiar with it at all."

"How familiar are you with vampires?" Hannah blurted while tracing the knots in the table.

The nun clasped her crucifix necklace and made the sign of the cross. "Is that the demon you speak of? Are you afraid that a vampire is after you?"

Hannah tilted her head to the side. "I *know* a vampire is after me. Or rather, I'm told, he's after the necklace I purchased from the Accademia Museum."

She spent the next twenty-five minutes slowly explaining everything with Maria's help. Maria spoke of what her ancestors had to say, while she told the nun what Val's family had to say. She told her about the channeling, too, but she said nothing about the seduction; although, she could see the question burning in the nun's eyes.

Hannah looked at her and bit her lip, waiting for her to speak. Sister Catherine bowed her head with her hands clasped in front of her and whispered something in Italian. When she was finished, she and Maria both made the cross sign over their chests. Hannah shot Maria a questioning glance, so the woman explained that Sister Catherine had said a prayer for her.

"Oh, thanks," she mumbled to the nun. "What do you think? I mean, can you help me?"

The nun looked at her with woeful eyes. She reached out and placed a gentle hand on her forearm. "I'm afraid I don't know what to do other than pray for your soul. Father Patrick might know more, however, so I will speak to him discretely on your behalf."

Hannah forced a feeble smile. "Thank you. I appreciate that." When she rose from the chair, the nun clasped her arm to halt her.

"Please be careful, and use the knowledge of your friends to assist you. And, of course, don't forget to pray." Her voice was soft and full of concern.

Hannah smiled at her. "I will pray non-stop if it will help."

"It always helps." She rose from her chair to walk the ladies out. "I'll call you at the hotel if Father Patrick has any advice or if he wants to see you."

Hannah nodded. "Thank you, Sister."

When they were outside, Maria gave her a sympathetic look. "I'm sorry that she couldn't help. Hopefully, Father Patrick will know something she doesn't. There has to be an answer somewhere."

Hannah appreciated the woman's optimism. "I guess I'll find some in the book Val is reading to me. And speaking of Val, I'm surprised I've not heard from him." She looked at her watch and saw that it was already a few minutes after 6:00. She checked her phone to make sure she didn't have a missed call or message, but she didn't. "I'm going to go back to my room to practice what I've already learned before he comes by. Thank you for listening to me and introducing me to Sister Catherine."

"Of course, Hannah. I wish you well, and please let me know if there's anything else I can do. I think I'll pick Diego's brain in the morning to see if he knows anything else about the legend."

"That's a great idea," she acknowledged. *Of course, I have to survive tonight first.*

She chose to walk back to the hotel instead of taking a taxi, even though it looked like a storm was coming. The rain breeze rustled her hair and sent an electric current through her nerves, which were more on edge than ever before in her life. She looked around at the happy tourists and locals, wondering what they would think if they only knew what was lurking in their city. Then the overwhelming sense of responsibility for their well-being washed over her, and she started to weep.

An elderly woman approached her and asked, "Mi scusi, signora, perché piangi?"

Hannah blinked the tears away and explained that she didn't speak Italian.

The woman put a hand to her chest and replied in English, "I said, excuse me, miss, why do you cry?"

"Oh, it's a long and complicated story," Hannah replied with a shudder.

The woman shook her head with a slight smile and pointed to a store front behind her. Hannah looked and saw a glowing hand-shaped sign in the window.

"I'm a fortune teller," the woman explained. "I can see the path you need to take, and that's why I came outside.

Hannah sniveled, "You can?"

The elderly woman nodded this time. "Si. I'm Serena, and I can tell you your future."

"Hi, Serena. My name is Hannah, and it's nice to meet you. May I ask what exactly brought you outside? I mean, what path?"

Serena took Hannah's left hand in hers and patted it. "The path that will save you from vampires."

Hannah's jaw dropped, and she found herself speechless. "How do…how…How do you know?"

"Come, let's go inside," Serena suggested with a smug grin and tugged on her hand.

She followed the woman into the mystical shop. She saw animal skulls, crystals, amulets, talismans, Ouija boards, and colorful herbs and powders. Serena led her behind a black curtain to a table containing a crystal ball and gestured for her to sit.

The woman waved her hands over the ball and chanted something in Italian before telling her, "I see an ancient prophecy in play. Four hundred years ago, it was said that a vampire would come awake again when the earth would shake and spill."

"The avalanche?" Hannah softly questioned.

With a nod, Serena continued, "I see a strong warrior with a pure heart. The warrior is meant to battle the undead, but something might get in his way."

"What?" Hannah scooted forward in her chair to examine the crystal ball. Of course, she couldn't see anything. "What might get in the way?"

Serena focused her dark eyes on her. "Love."

Hannah shot out of her chair like a bottle rocket. "What? Love for whom?"

Serena focused back on the ball while swirling tea leaves in a mug. She examined both carefully before finally answering, "It is unclear at this time because three hearts are involved."

Hannah narrowed her eyes. "But I thought you see the future."

The woman smiled at her, causing fine lines to form around her mouth. "That part is unclear because of free will. You haven't decided yet."

Hannah's hand flew to her chest. "Me?" she shrieked. "I've not decided what?"

Serena tilted her head. "Whom you love."

Hannah threw money on the small table and fled from the shop with tears burning her eyes. She ran the rest of the way back to her hotel, passing several curious looky loos on the sidewalk and in the hotel lobby.

She ran up the stairwell to her room and to the safe. She yanked the necklace out, cupping the cold jewel in her hands.

"Help me. Show me what I have to do," she pleaded with the gem.

She closed her eyes because her head began to spin. She took several deep breaths to calm her nerves and stomach while trying to find clarity where there was confusion.

"Love? Am I supposed to love Val, or even worse, is she saying I'm falling for a vampire?"

A shadow suddenly encased her, so she opened her eyes and ran to the window. She had the drapes open, but the sky was growing black from the brewing storm, blanketing out the sinking sun. Thunder rumbled overhead, and lightening made the black clouds glow.

She paced the small room. It was so dark out already, and nightfall was coming soon. *Where is Val?* For once, she really needed to see the warrior.

She was still holding the necklace, so she slipped it over her head and pulled her hair through. She needed to find a connection with it, and she needed to do it right then. She looked at the sky again, which was even blacker than before, and clutched the amulet.

"You have to work. I can't become a vampire, and I don't want to die," she whispered to the necklace.

She picked up her phone and dialed Val's number.

"Hello?" a woman's voice answered.

Hannah looked at her phone to make sure she dialed the right number, and she had. "Um, hello, this is Hannah Rowen. Is Val there?"

"Hello, dear. This is Anna, Val's mother. I'm afraid he was injured today, and so he's sleeping."

"Oh, what happened?"

The woman sighed. "Well, I'm not exactly sure, but it appears that something fell from an old building and hit him in the head. Anyway, he has a concussion, so he's on bed rest."

"I'm sorry to hear that," Hannah offered and paced her room as a loud clash of thunder rattled the window and her nerves.

"I realize that doesn't help—"

Hannah didn't hear what the rest of Anna's sentence was because she dropped the phone when she realized she suddenly had company in her room. Armand was approaching her like a quiet fog rolling in.

She backed away until she bumped into the bed. She looked out the window for a ray of hope, but the remaining daylight was swallowed up by the thunderstorm. Panic burned through her veins. She had no escape from his seductive clutches. He would do whatever it was he wanted to do to her. When he licked his lips, she wondered what he'd do first.

Will he seduce me or bite me?

Armand stood close enough to her to feel the heat coming off her body and to hear her heart pounding erratically. The sudden storm gave him the perfect opportunity to finish what he'd started. The full moon would be up in a couple of hours, and in the meantime, he could enjoy her sweet flesh.

"I've come for you, my beauty, like I said I would," he growled. "I'm glad to find you alone."

She forgot she was against the bed already and tried to back up. Her legs buckled, and she fell backward onto the springy mattress, which made him show off his vampire grin.

With a chuckle, he informed her, "That's right, my beauty. First, I'm going to *fuck* you like a beast in heat." He stepped closer to the bed.

In a shaky voice, she threatened, "Val will be here any minute, and he'll stop you."

Armand laughed again, and it sounded like one hundred degrees of evil. "No he won't. I took care of that problem already."

Her brows pulled together. "*You* hurt him?"

He casually waved a hand. "Well, my lackey did, but it was at my behest." He pulled his shirt off and climbed into the bed while she tried to scramble away. "Tonight is different, my pretty. Tonight, there are no hypnotic chants. You'll give yourself to me because you know it's what you want"—he leaned in until his lips were centimeters away from hers—"You desire this as much as I do. Surrender to your temptations."

When she opened her mouth to protest, to scream, to do anything but accept what was coming, he thrust his tongue inside and swallowed her up. While he molested her mouth and groped her body, she squeezed her eyes shut and concentrated on channeling. She fought to imagine the energy shield that should be protecting her. She pictured the necklace, which wasn't doing anything to help her yet, and tried to pull everything together inside herself to connect with it. His mouth had moved to her neck, and she felt his fangs grazing her skin.

It's now or never.

Her body felt warm, and it wasn't just from the passion his touch and the press of his hard shaft was igniting. She felt her hands tingling as they tried to push him off. It was hard to focus, but she fought to resist his advances, and finally, she felt something strong inside herself that hadn't been there before. A sudden light made her eyelids fly open. There was a red glow coming from her chest, and she realized it was the necklace.

I'm connected…

She stared into his red eyes, glowing in the light of the jewel, and pushed him with a strength she didn't have before. "Go fuck yourself!" she screamed as he flew off her. She scrambled from the bed and ran for the door, but he was there in a flash, bracing himself against it.

"So, you want to play games?" he taunted and reached for her as she tried to scramble away.

Hannah concentrated on her aura, trying to form an impenetrable shield that he couldn't break. Then she heard something that did break—the door as Val came crashing through it.

He charged at Armand with something wielded in his hand. She couldn't make it out until lightning streaked the sky and filled the room with its iridescent glow. It was a steel crucifix with a bladed end.

The agile vampire deflected him and flung him across the room into the wall with a heavy thud. Then he pounced on top of him.

"Use the jewel!" Val grunted. "It's up to you!"

Hannah watched in horror as Armand wrapped a meaty hand around Val's neck while his other hand delivered a crushing blow to his face. When he reached back to strike again, she grabbed his wrist and yanked him off the warrior.

Surprise was registered on the vampire's handsome face. He sprang to his feet and approached her while she backed away. He licked his lips and burned holes in her with his red eyes.

"Come with me, my beauty. Be my love for all eternity." He reached a beckoning hand for her. "We'll live forever, making passionate love all night long. You can be my immortal bride and queen to the undead."

Hannah glanced toward Val's motionless body. It was up to her to end this, or she would become Armand's prisoner forever. She dug inside herself for the courage she needed.

"No thanks. I don't think death is a good look for me."

She heard something in her mind then. It was a chant in another language. *Arabic?* She couldn't translate the words, but somehow, she knew exactly what they were telling her to do. She clasped the necklace with her left hand and held her right hand out. She repeated the strange words as she heard them, and the most incredible thing happened. He stopped walking toward her and screamed in agony while wrapping his arms around himself.

Val regained consciousness and rushed to her side, throwing his arm around her and backing away from the screeching vampire. He threw the crucifix dagger into Armand's chest, and the vampire instantly crumpled to the floor in a pile of ashes.

"I told you that you could do it. I knew you were strong enough," he stated and squeezed her against him.

Hannah looked at the handsome Italian and smiled. "Yes, you're very smart. Now, shut up and kiss me."

All the stress of the past several days melted away as his lips engulfed hers. She felt more alive than ever, and she knew just how to celebrate. She broke off the kiss, grabbed her phone, and called into work to leave a message that she was taking her remaining week of vacation. She'd not given the man, or love for that matter, a fair chance, and now was the time to rectify that.

"So, you're going to stay in Italy for another week then?" Val asked with a big smile.

She winked at him. "No, not exactly. I'm going to use my frequent flyer miles to take you to New York with me. You showed me your land, so let me show you mine."

He pulled her in for another kiss just as there was a knock on the door.

"Miss Rowen? It's the hotel manager. Neighboring guests said they heard screaming from your room. Are you all right? Do I need to call the authorities for you?"

Hannah flipped on the light and opened the door for the man. "Yes, everything is fine. We just had a little... fight."

Confused, he looked at Val, the pile of ash on the floor, and then back to her. "Damn vampires. They always leave such a mess," he mumbled and walked away.

Twenty-five

The magical week was over, and it was time to drive Val to the airport. She'd taken him on tours all over the city, including the MET, where she received some curious looks from her co-workers. She'd taken him on multiple tours of her bedroom too. The sex was much better than the first time, and the wow factor was always present, but it was time to say goodbye. She knew she'd miss him too. It felt good to have a "normal" life again; although, she'd certainly never forget all that had happened in Italy. It was just a shame that she couldn't tell her family and friends that she'd saved the world from vampires.

"So, Valentino, thank you for your help, and I hope you enjoyed your time in America," she said at his gate.

He smiled a boyish grin. "I enjoyed my time with you, even if it did get messy." He reached up to touch his face where his olive skin was still bluish from Armand's blow.

She nodded. "Well, I think you might get to see more of me in the very near future, and that should go smoother."

"Oh, are you planning another visit already?" He smiled hopefully and squeezed her hand.

She tilted her head and returned his smile. "Kind of. The Accademia Museum has offered me the job of head curator, and it would be hard to turn down." In fact, it was impossible to turn down, and she'd already accepted the offer. Her return flight was in five days.

I hope you enjoyed my story. Please leave a review on Amazon and/or Goodreads.

♥